the SMASH!

James Harbridge

Pen Press Publishers Ltd

First published in Great Britain by
Pen Press Publishers Ltd
25 Eastern Place
Brighton
BN2 1GJ

ISBN13: 978-1-906206-77-2

Printed and bound in the UK by
Cpod, Trowbridge, Wiltshire

A catalogue record of this book is available from
 the British Library

Cover photography by Scott Murray; model: Sam Parker
Cover design by Jacqueline Abromeit

Introduction

"My mother, the late great tennis champion Maureen "Little Mo" Connolly, won Wimbledon in 1952, 1953 and 1954. How she revered those hallowed grounds at the All England Lawn Tennis & Croquet Club! James Harbridge has penned a riveting thriller utilizing the Wimbledon Championships as a dazzling backdrop of intrigue, murder and action. Harbridge is an intelligent and crafty writer who combines his deep passions for tennis and crime fiction to create a murder mystery novel that totally enthrals his reader. The author is a master wordsmith who designs an emotional labyrinth of schemes, betrayals and jealousies that, in turn, propel his characters to manoeuvre for position and power. Whew! "The Smash!" will take your breath away! Harbridge emerges the champion in this fast-paced, clever and fun read!"

Cindy Brinker Simmons
President
Maureen Connolly Brinker Tennis Foundation

Prologue

Hi,

"The Smash!" is fiction, a thriller – the fruit of the writer's imagination – so it shouldn't be taken too seriously!

But happily, as a professional tennis player, I couldn't put it down when I read an early draft of it in September 2006, whilst on the train from Brighton to Queen's Club in West Kensington. I found it to be really good.

The various worldwide locations in "The Smash!" reflect the sport's international nature, but ultimately the crucial action takes place at Wimbledon's All England Club. That's only natural as it remains unique, the home of tennis. I never knew, when I took up the game via school friends in 1997, that I would make my debut there eight years later, competing in the juniors and beating a Russian girl. And now my goal is to hopefully be a perennial performer at the Championships because I'd love to exhibit my serve and volley, attacking style right there on Centre Court in exciting singles encounters, delighting the crowds. We have all struggled and fought to make it to Wimbledon, but I love the challenges of this sport, the hard work of it and the drama it creates.

continued...

I'm glad James is trying to enhance the popularity of tennis, and particularly the women's game. He has worked hard to create this whodunit, and I am sure you are going to enjoy it as much as I did.

Best wishes,

Natasha Khan

Chapter 1

"I hope "The Smash!" is almost as good as my 1980s thrillers, "Tie-Break" and "The Net"!"

- Ilie Nastase, Wimbledon's
Men's Finalist, 1972 and 1976

TERRY PROUDLEY was a man with a secret.

But he wasn't about to share it with anyone, because that would be too dangerous.

He had to maintain his visible demeanour of being a solid, uncomplicated soul. He was determined to do so.

To the outside world, he was indeed an unspectacular figure, but nonetheless he hovered on the fringes of that which eternally gripped England, namely the world of fame and fortune.

Terry, about 35 years old, with scruffy, spiky hair and an inclination to being a little overweight, had somehow put aside his natural insecurities to become tennis correspondent on the new London nightly paper, The Evening Echo. And as today was the start of the Wimbledon Championships, he was to be envied, if only for a fortnight. Terry would be able to enjoy every day of the extravaganza, with the ability to survey Centre Court or Court No 1 or any other court he cared to see, coupled with access to the practice sessions and the plethora of press conferences involving all the stars, who would have to address his probing questions, whether they liked it or not.

And as far as he was concerned, the best part was that this did not feel like a job at all. He had followed the game avidly from a young age, and had reported on professional tennis (albeit mostly on a freelance basis) for all of his adult life - ever since that epoch-making moment when he had walked out of law school.

Accordingly, he had the ability to pay scant attention to the game, whilst still satisfying his editor with prose which, although a little pedestrian, could not really be questioned.

The previous June week had seen Terry, oddly confident wearing rock star shades, relaxing in five star splendour at Eastbourne's imposing Grand Hotel. He was blessed with a suite overlooking the sun-kissed sea.

The great and the good of women's pro tennis had been at the South Coast to battle it out on the lush lawns of Devonshire Park.

Terry sipped his coffee daily in the hotel's inspiring chandelier-bedecked breakfast hall, and he watched the sport's multi-millionairesses file in one by one, preparing for another day at their "office".

First to arrive each sunrise was, appropriately, the world No 1 from Florida, diminutive Holly Fleming. She appeared relaxed as an over-attentive waiter ushered her to a private corner table whilst she continued chatting on her mobile to her fiancé, the newly crowned men's world No 1, England's Javea Jackson. Her immaculate all white tracksuit outfit was testimony to her awesome athleticism, and her creamy skin was unblemished. She boasted a coiffure of short, shiny, tight black curls.

Terry overheard her laughing and giggling on the 'phone about last minute arrangements for the couple's planned mid-July wedding, and he now felt certain that, whatever his earlier doubts, this duo would never be broken by anyone or anything.

Holly, a 21 year-old who slugged out every match from the baseline, arose from her seat when the call was finished and sauntered over to the breakfast buffet, choosing a bowl of low fat strawberry yoghurt and a banana.

Behind her, the doubles specialist (or *attempted* specialist) from Austria, golden-haired Adele Schmidt, came jogging into the room, and raised each of her upper arms - first right, then left - to her respective rosy cheeks to wipe away accumulated beads of sweat. Her T-shirt was close fitting and black, and she wore figure-hugging black shorts, too. The same overly obliging waiter ushered the slim but bow-legged star to a reserved table - this one on the other side of the banquet area. Immediately, insolent Adele, full of contrived bravado, loudly ordered a chilled glass of fresh orange juice from the hapless worker.

Terry smiled to himself because Holly, seeing that Adele had a prime table looking out to sea, instantaneously admonished the waiter and insisted that tomorrow she should be given Adele's spot. The server scuttled away, muttering something about checking with his boss, instinctively mindful that retreat was his best form of defence. Holly and Adele studiously avoided each other, preferring - whenever necessary - to look at the high ceiling above.

Terry mused on the fact that the waiter's defensive skills neatly mirrored Adele's own. Adele had a reputation of being a dour, humourless player who lacked the innate guts to attack opponents. She relied on her heavily underspun backhand to grind down the opposition meaning that, while she rarely made an error, she was equally rare in creating a winning shot. As a result, her matches became long wars of mind-numbing attrition which caused spectators to rush for the exits. Then, with time, tomboyish Adele lost that yard of pace essential for good singles play, and so here she now was, grimly fighting on, but only in the (somewhat unfounded) hope that her career would enjoy an Indian summer and some measure of real success on the doubles court.

Terry couldn't help but marvel at Adele's obsessive zeal, especially when all the signs suggested that the Austrian would soon be forgotten by the fans once she fell into retirement.

The same could not be said of "leggy Angela from Amsterdam", as Terry was apt to label the six-footer Angela de Jong, who was, strangely enough, from Amsterdam. The Dutch girl waltzed in, showing off her hazel brown flowing tresses. She was resplendent in a bright red t-shirt and matching micro shorts. Angela was the world No 2; finals across the globe increasingly pitted this very sexy and chilled celebrity against the relentlessly ferocious Holly Fleming.

Terry noticed that both Angela and Holly automatically stiffened as soon as they found the other in their own supposed star territory. It happened each day at the Grand in Eastbourne; neither diva could bear to catch even a half-glance of the other.

In contrast, world No 3, 18 year-old Jacalyn Jeanice from Paris bounced daily into breakfast, with her dalmatian puppy Amour tucked under her tanned arm. Jacalyn, of medium height, said a "bonjour" to everyone, including Terry, for whom she always seemed to reserve a small, slightly sardonic, knowing smile. Only curvy Jacalyn, among these sports people, wore "street apparel"; she favoured a jaw-dropping tiny black dress, which exquisitely displayed her perfect figure. But the talk on tour often revolved around whether she was a bottle blonde and whether her blue eyes were simply a result of cosmetic contact lenses. Besides, her bee-stung lips were collagen-created, according to the scoffers.

The *joie de vivre* of vibrant Jacalyn clashed markedly with the last main player to appear, the British world No 4, frail and small Natalie Sloane who was skimpily clad in a garish yellow and blue, tight ensemble which revealed blatantly her flat stomach and lean legs. She mumbled an apologetic "sorry" as she seemed to stumble into the room, and her eyes never left the shoelaces of her expensive trainers. Terry contemplated Natalie's puffy face and mousy hair with some sympathy; since her big breakthrough on the circuit, she had gained fame but inconsistency on court. Outwardly she was now a pale shadow of her former self; the darkness of her visage seemed to be some kind of warning mask that uttered "do not get close". The other tennis girls whispered behind Natalie's back that this self-disgust was no doubt divine retribution for a foe who could be, in the words of one, "an arrogant, heartless, cold bitch".

Most of the time, the atmosphere in the Grand's breakfast hall was studied, semi-silent and tense, but that environment broke one morning when sleazy agent Drew L Todd - an American who was anything but clean-cut - briskly walked in and moved over to where his client Jacalyn was sitting. Suddenly, the usually calm white and black spotted Amour careered forward from its chair, barking loudly and abruptly, desperate to bite the unfortunate New Yorker.

The whole room burst into laughter. The players don't really like sports agents, Terry reminded himself.

By the end of the Eastbourne tournament, it was just Holly and Jacalyn in for breakfast, along with journalists such as Terry, who later reported (in part):

"American ace Holly Fleming put the icing on her cake of Wimbledon preparations with a straight sets finals' thrashing here in Eastbourne of beautiful rival Jacalyn Jeanice.

With English starlet Natalie Sloane crashing out in the first round, we had anticipated that the duel for the seaside crown would feature Holly against leggy world No 2, Angela de Jong.

But Parisien moppet Jacalyn Jeanice put paid to that proposition in the semis, and now Holly has demolished the French sensation 6-2, 6-2."

And so, against this backdrop of egos, rivalries and pressure, the magic of Wimbledon was about to be revealed yet again.

Chapter 2

On the first day of Wimbledon - correction, on the first *morning* of Wimbledon - Holly Fleming knew that something bad was happening. Even the previous night's dinner at her favourite Indian restaurant in London SW19 had failed to lift her spirits.

Her parents were stressing her by even being in the country, and it was intolerable that the three of them were in this huge rented detached residence in Marryat Road, close to the courts of Wimbledon's All England Club. Mom and Dad's ostensible motive was to be present when Holly won her first Wimbledon title, but Holly reckoned that in truth they wanted to derail her upcoming marriage to British heart-throb, 18 year-old Javea.

Yes, she would admit that Javea could be difficult and moody and, yes, he liked to get his own way (like nearly all successful pro athletes). But the media and paparazzi were after him night and day, and the fans were too demanding. After all, it had been 1936 since the previous British Wimbledon men's singles Champion. Sadly, the watching chavs who now wore Fred Perry attire had no knowledge of who or what Fred Perry had ever been.

Holly's sullen brooding about her parents' failure to warm to Javea subsided in milliseconds when she heard the letterbox of the oak front door click open. She sprung from her bed, rushed downstairs and picked up the tabloid newspaper from the doormat ... only to be sickened by what she saw. Holly's boyfriend was there on page one, leering happily into a camera that had no doubt been thrust too close to his face. His eyes were cast in a sideways direction and the paper had printed opposite him a photo of some cheeky girl sticking her pierced tongue out with pride. Around her neck was a flashy gold necklace broadcasting "J4L".

Holly's stomach turned gruelling somersaults as the banner headline swam in and out of focus: "LOVE IN THE SKIES: AIR HOSTESS BEDS CHAMP JAVEA".

Somehow, Holly coerced herself into taking some gulps of air; she fought for steadiness and stability as she read on:

"DEFENDING WIMBLEDON CHAMP JAVEA JACKSON, 18, has been having a tempestuous affair with part-time air hostess Larissa LaDame, we can reveal.

And his antics with daring Larissa are sure to land him in hot water with his tennis star fiancée, the usually ice-cool assassin Holly Fleming.

We were unable to get any response from Holly's exclusive rented Wimbledon property when we tried to break the news last night.

Stunning Larissa readily admits that she went all out to ensnare sports hero Javea - but adds that she never expected that he would yield to her charms.

Says Larissa: 'My story is an important one as other girl-friends of top celebrities need to know that these guys cannot be trusted. I mean, I am just an ordinary female and no-one could have imagined that Javea would have wanted me.'

LaDame's revelations are set to rock the staid All England Club with other male stars surely concerned that additional kiss and tell exposés from various sources may be imminent.

We hope today to sign up Larissa LaDame on a world exclusive basis, and then you can read all this week - only in these pages - about increasingly intimate revelations and her amazing experiences with champ Javea."

Holly threw the paper to one side. She was dizzy and sweating. She knew Javea, for all his complexity, was meant to be her life partner. Could it be that her parents' disdain had led him to be unfaithful? But how could he so cruelly damage her? And during

Wimbledon? Had he simply become so sure of himself that he thought the papers would not find out about such an escapade? Worse still, had he even fallen a little in love with this low-down tramp, this purported Larissa? How could she summon the strength to play her match tomorrow? All Holly wanted to do was crawl into a corner and die ... and yet, and yet that was not the Holly Fleming way at all.

The tiny star commanded herself to get back on her feet. Adversity is good, she told herself. I am lucky to have a problem that needs to be solved, she reasoned. Yes, Holly Fleming would not submit to a crisis. Whatever happens, the sun will come back up for me tomorrow, she avowed.

And with this renewed American optimism, Holly rushed back upstairs to her mobile, determined to summon Javea to an urgent summit to discuss their pending marriage. Ms Fleming was quietly certain that she would emerge from this scenario having had the last laugh.

A little later, Holly impatiently tore open an envelope addressed to her, which had also landed on the doormat, shortly after that horrific newspaper. It was a breathless fan letter - "...admire you greatly" ... "find you inspirational" ... and she tossed it in the kitchen bin without any thought.

Chapter 3

Terry read the same tabloid article whilst again breakfasting alone, this time in the fake French surroundings of Wimbledon Village's Café Rouge.

The story also made him mournful, but for an entirely different reason, which was bound up with professional esteem.

The whole world and his wife had been after Javea ever since his startling victory as a 17 year-old in the Wimbledon finals of the previous year, and Terry's editor - like every other editor - had demanded that a one-on-one interview be procured and unique insights obtained.

Terry had known Javea since the latter was a junior, but a Wimbledon winner can afford to pick and choose who he speaks to, and Terry could be a somewhat humdrum writer.

Nonetheless, Javea had to admire the persistence of the lowly hack who tracked him for many weeks.

Finally, one night - just over three months earlier, at the beginning of March - both Javea and Terry found a mutually opportune moment to nullify the cat and mouse game. A truce was reached.

They were both staying at the opulent five star Al Bustan Rotana Hotel in Dubai, where the elite of men's pro tennis were performing that week.

Terry could not sleep and the vast, lofty hotel atrium was nearly deserted as he sipped a double espresso there at 1am. His line of vision, by chance, was directed at the hotel's entrance doors. Tall Javea, with flowing blond locks, ambled back into the hotel after a late night stroll along the humid but prettily named Casablanca Street.

The eyes of the superstar and the everyman met momentarily, but there was a simultaneous recognition that now was as good a time as any to converse with the other.

Terry found it laughable that to obtain something approximating to a meaningful Javea Jackson worldwide Wimbledon exclusive, for June, he was reduced to begging his compatriot for five hurried minutes of chat in the United Arab Emirates - in March!

But he stood up from his half-finished coffee and warmly welcomed Javea with the words: "Ah, here he is! England's finest in a foreign land!"

Javea gave a lop-sided grin. "Mr Proudley, a pleasure to meet you."

"At long last," retorted Terry, but without malice.

"So it's 1am at night, right, and you want me to give a press conference, huh?" deadpanned Javea.

"Javea, you know how it is. You're England's finest sportsman. We all need something slightly original to satisfy our editors. I just thought …"

"That I could help you out."

"You see, I'd be very much obliged."

"Shoot," said Javea, falling into the comfortable sofa. "A Perrier?" he enquired of the advancing Thai waitress.

"Like I say," Terry started nervously, "I am looking for a new angle on the Javea Jackson which the British public already knows, and has already fallen in love with!"

"Don't tell Holly that; she's already a bit jealous."

"Oh, I see. Rather, I don't. Why is that?"

"Partly just because of tennis. Y'know how it is, most of the year the men's circuit plays at completely different places to the women's. Aside from the Grand Slams - Melbourne, Paris, Wimbledon, New York - we hardly meet."

"And what's your take on marriage?"

Javea roared with laughter. "Oh no, Terry, you're not in the big boys' league, mate. All the personal introspection stuff goes to the highest bidder. I'm not about to open up my entire private life just like that; you're gonna have to accept that."

"I do, of course, Javea. I have every respect for you. But so much has already been written about you. You had an unhappy childhood. You were determined to make good. You were orphaned by the age of nine when your parents were the victims of a terrible car crash. You turned to tennis. It was your only soul mate. You progressed rapidly through the ranks and then, last year, bang! You astonished us all by capturing the Wimbledon title even though you were only entered as a wild card. What would you now write if you were in my shoes?"

"That none of the above tells much about me," ventured Javea. "And please don't recycle those stories about my love of white toast and marmalade as a pre-match meal of choice! You cannot believe how many pots of marmalade are sent to me each week by fans everywhere I play!"

"So give me more," implored Terry.

"That, I am not about to do. Just because I can hit a ball over a net better than virtually everyone doesn't mean my brain should be fodder for a psychoanalyst."

The Perrier water arrived. Silence fell on the pair.

"But I will tell you a little about my tactics for Wimbledon," proffered the 18 year-old.

Terry groaned inwardly. The technical aspects of tennis were of little interest to his readers who only really wanted to know what happened to the greats away from the courts.

"I shall chip and charge a lot more this year. Last time out I was naive and played too much from the baseline. Not this time. I've learned my lesson. I'll slice my backhand returns and rush to the net and hit some crap volleys for winners! I'm gonna be more aggressive and take my chances. None of us know how long we have got in the game," he added, a trifle morbidly.

"Will love affect your chances?"

"My tennis and Holly are two completely separate things. So no, I'm still gonna be me," came the truculent riposte. "And I'm not talking more about her. And look, now you've got a bit of info, Terry. 'Javea's tactical plans laid bare ... etc, etc.' Surely that's enough from me?"

But Jackson could see in Terry's eyes that the journalist hungered for more. And whilst it was late and the player was tired, he had to admit he had a feeling of sensitivity for anyone forced to toil at his career in the middle of the night. Besides, Javea was lonely. He knew no-one in Dubai and lacked any desire that week to make new acquaintances.

"Tell you what," Javea said casually, "let me give you something off the record."

"Thanks, but really, what's the point of me knowing something that I can never use without worrying that you may sue me?"

"I don't know," admitted Javea. "I just think you'll be interested. And, y'know, if my flight out of here goes down in the Arabian Sea or something, you'll have a gilt-edged story right there in front of you."

"Hmm," responded Terry. "That does sound a bit interesting, though heaven forbid anything should happen to you, Javea. You're not going anywhere off this mortal coil! So what can you share with me? Off the record, of course."

There was a second's stillness. "I'm writing a book," Javea confided triumphantly.

"Who are you writing it with?" enquired Terry, managing to sound selfish, wounded, despondent and gloomy - all at the same time.

"No-one; it'll be an autobiography, Terry. That way I can really get my point across."

"And what is it that you are burning to tell? I thought you just said that your private life was exactly that - private."

"The book's not going to be about me."

"An autobiography that's not about you? I don't follow."

Javea smiled. "The book will give me the chance to get even with a few people. To settle a few scores with those that have wronged me in tennis. Oh, don't misunderstand me, the game's given me a lot already, but this sport is a sad sport in many ways and many of the people involved in it are corrupt. See, now I've said it - well, off the record. The corruption in tennis is never spoken about, and I'm the Wimbledon Champion now and can do something to correct it."

"Who's to blame?"

"Who's not to blame?"

"Come on, Javea, give me something that I didn't know. For instance, you guys never respect the agents, do you. Is that why you split with Drew L Todd and now do all your own deals? I thought he got you a huge bunch of endorsements before you even stepped on Centre Court for the first time."

"You'll have to read the book. He'll be in there, all right. You could say he wrecked my life. OK, maybe I'm being overly emotional. However, now it's payback time for Mr Drew."

"What exactly happened?"

"Can't say," pouted Javea. "In the book that guy's complete lack of morality will be totally exposed."

"And has he any idea of your resentment?"

"Absolutely. When I sacked him I made it perfectly clear why I was doing it. And he knows I have something on him that could destroy him. What's more, I recently told him that what he's trying to hide will soon find its way into my book."

"Aren't you worried he'll try to sully your name? Or seek redress through the courts for defamation?"

"Bring it on! Let's see him do his best, Terry. I'll be waiting. And he won't win, anyway. Because right is on my side."

"But you can't base your book on your hatred for one of tennis' best known figures, Javea. You might be justified in whatever you are going to say, but will the public back you for a vitriolic attack on the guy?"

"Ha! It won't just be him. In fact, some of the players are just as bad, some of the female players in fact."

"Who?"

"Well, did you know that one of the smartest stars on the women's circuit has been having an affair behind her boyfriend's back with one of the top umpires? Doesn't that stink? Favours off court for favours on the court! And perhaps she's involved with other officials, too!"

"You're seriously suggesting that an umpire would side on close calls with a player due to some relationship he may be covertly having with her? But that's absurd!"

"Not at all, Terry. You know as well as I do that in a tight final set the difference between winning and losing can come down to the odd decision here or there. Hawk-Eye, the new ball tracking technology, makes no difference. Besides, they often only allow you a couple of challenges via Hawk-Eye per set, and not every tournament and every court has Hawk-Eye anyway. So having an official in your back pocket, whether he is the chair umpire or simply a linesjudge, could make all the difference."

"So who is this femme fatale?"

Javea looked around the desolate hotel atrium, but although he saw no-one close by, he still declined to say anything. Instead, he spied a cheap ballpoint pen which had been abandoned at a neighbouring table. He took it in his hand, and pulled a piece of paper from his jeans pocket. Seeing that one side was conveniently blank, he tore a strip from it and wrote down the name of a female tennis star, then passed it to Terry.

Terry read the name. "I don't believe it!" he murmured. "Whatever you say, can it really be true?"

"And she's not the only one," retaliated Javea, with temptation in his voice. "The fact is that I saw her coming out of Jon Smartson's hotel room in the dead of night at, I forget the place, oh yes, it was in Melbourne or somewhere."

"But Smartson's one of Britain's most respected umpires. How could he ever get himself mixed up in such a scandal?"

"You see, Terry, you're a journalist, but sadly you're also a dreamer. You never look beyond the book's cover. I've always known that guy is not to be trusted."

"In fact, now I recall, didn't you two have a disagreement in Las Vegas?"

"Yeah, I made a mistake there. Smartson kept calling me for foot-faults and no-one ever foot-faults me. He did it to me again in a third set tie-breaker and I threw my racket down. The guy hit me with a warning. I was mental with anger and I let rip at him - I wish I hadn't - 'One day the world's gonna know all about you!' It was a crazy thing to do - and I got a penalty point against me. Thank God I went on to win."

"Forgive me, Javea. Are you saying that in front of five thousand fans or something you publicly threatened to expose Smartson for sleeping with a top female pro? Your words could have got you banned for a year or more!"

"True: but I knew what I said was true. So I also knew that Smartson would be too gutless to report me - which means I got away scot-free."

"And did the female player in question ever take you to task for nearly sharing her private moments with an entire stadium?"

Javea laughed. The reporter merely sat puzzled. "Terry," he laughed again. "She probably saw me when leaving that hotel room, but you really do misunderstand, mate. The incident in Las Vegas happened *before* what I saw in Melbourne!"

"I don't understand," agreed Terry uncomfortably. "What do you mean?"

"Smartson knew full well that I was referring to an earlier thing involving him. And what it was - and I obtained this quite by chance from a good source close to the horse's mouth - was an audacious three-party attempt to destroy the very fabric of tennis! Ha! I sound like a journo now, Terry."

"You do, but you're losing me. What are you referring to?"

"Do you remember a yesteryear female talent called Blanca Alessandra? Of course you do - better than I do. Alessandra was before my time. Anyways, in her day she was amazing looking, and you know what that always means? Stalkers! She was a tall, slim girl, and one year she went to India and played somewhere like Mumbai. It turned out that her match was watched by some young Bollywood film star who either was a mafioso or was closely connected to India's criminal underworld. This guy, Karan, was obsessed with Alessandra and began literally following her from tournament to tournament. She couldn't get rid of him! And eventually she fell for him and he told her that it was his life's fantasy to see her win a Grand Slam. It's true, she was near the top of the tree at the time, a Grand Slam was not beyond her. But the mafioso was used to simply buying things or 'making them happen'. He bribed Smartson to fall in with his plan and after that other high-ranking officials were offered bribes and there were threats made against Alessandra's rivals. Karan was actually trying to buy Alessandra a Grand Slam victory! The umpires' co-operation was bought to call close balls in her favour (there was no Hawk-Eye at all back then!) and Karan threatened other, specific prolific players with dire consequences if they had it in mind to defeat Alessandra."

"But she never won a Grand Slam," interjected Terry.

"No, because I guess the enormity and the shame of the scam hit Alessandra. I was playing as a junior around then at the same club where she was practising. I found her one day in tears in the corridor outside the locker rooms. I asked her what was wrong and she looked at me and crumbled. I was so young, so scared. Earlier in the week she had been very happy to talk. She urged me to play in the Channel Islands, in Jersey, at least once. She talked of staying at a hotel there in a bay and said it had been the happiest place she'd ever been. 'I'd like to live there every day,' she said. But in the end Alessandra simply vanished from tennis and everyone glossed over it, saying that she had family problems in Venezuela or the Maldives or somewhere - she certainly had a mixed parentage!"

"So this gangster drove Alessandra from the game she loved?"

"If in fact she ever did love it. No-one with true ethics would go anywhere near a match fixing set-up. My sympathy for her is non-existent. But what I really regret is letting slip to Smartson my knowledge about all this. The gangster Karan certainly knew how to enforce silence from the officials he bribed and the players he threatened. And they keep quiet because the thing never came to fruition anyway. But it'll be in my book cos cheating, even attempted cheating, destroys me. I wish, though, that Smartson hadn't had advanced warning of my plans. My guess is that by now both Alessandra and Karan will know what's in store; he'll be real angry and Alessandra will be determined to stop her reputation from being permanently destroyed."

"So why are you doing this, Javea? Surely playing tennis is your primary focus right now, along with arranging married life with Holly. Where does any of this take you?"

"Like I say," responded Javea, "life's meant to be interesting and this is my way of making sure it is! There are too many bad people spoiling this game and I intend to bring that to an end. Why should I sit back and allow these people to prosper?"

"Look, Javea, it's late. You need to rest for your match tomorrow. But think carefully about putting all these things in a book where they are out in the open with your enemies lining up to malign you. And besides, in any book there has to be some humour!"

"Humour," said Javea, echoing Terry, and trying the word out for size. "Well, I am gonna name the female player who has had a big crush on me since the junior days and can't accept the fact that I'm not interested in her! And, yes, I shall say who the female is that hates me all because of mixed doubles! What else? Terry, you'll understand I have to tell the readers about the girl on the circuit who's taking recreational drugs and maybe performance enhancers too!"

"You're pulling my leg, now, Javea. Come on. Those three things can't all be true. Are you sure your book's not fiction?" Terry smiled at the famous face opposite him.

"Oh no," came Javea's riposte as he suddenly got up and moved his glass to one side. With a steely glare, the star added: "This is all true, I assure you. And off the record. Highly confidential, remember."

Again, he found for the pen and quickly wrote down the names of three more stars of women's tennis. He held out the resultant scrap of paper to Terry who swallowed hard as he took and read it. In many ways, it would be better not to have this knowledge, thought Terry. The information Javea was providing could throw the world of tennis into a complete crisis.

Unbelievably, as Javea sat down again, there was even more. "One last thing will make your head spin, mate. Don't you agree that our sport needs turning upside down now and then? Y'know, old rivalries revived, renewed tensions on court, hostility at the changeovers! Well, perhaps not the hostility, but you know what I mean. So I am also going to use my book to breathe added oxygen into the women's game. And you'll have to agree with me that this idea is pure genius."

"Which is what?" quizzed Terry. "This all seems like total Russian roulette!"

"Well, I think it will be a fitting memory to my old coach, Stan Power. He was an all-time great, wasn't he? And yes, he only coached me for a few months before his death, but he was a larger than life character. Can you believe he trained so many of us top players?"

"Yes, in the last couple of years alone he worked on and off with Holly, and with Angela de Jong in Amsterdam, Jacalyn Jeanice in Paris and here in London with Natalie Sloane. All that before he spent those countless hours attempting to improve your forehand approach shot!"

"Whatever. But the man never shared anything he knew about one player when he came to coach their rival. So, if Holly asked about the tactical ways to overcome, say, Angela's game, the guy would just clam up and refuse to say anything. He would always maintain that he owed a duty of confidentiality whilst he was alive to each of his 'clients'. That kind of loyalty is so rare in tennis."

Terry was intrigued. "You mean he never shared knowledge gained about a former student with a current student? Didn't that annoy his current person, whomever it was from time to time?"

"Not really, because the guy brainwashed everyone to think only about themselves and how to maximise themselves. His argument was that success came from within and that the individual controlled his or her own destiny. But guess what?"

"Yes?" asked Terry, feeling ill at ease.

"He said that to keep the sponsors of women's tennis happy it would be great, once he died, if all his knowledge was laid bear to the entire world! All his aggregate wisdom about Holly's footwork or Natalie's second serve placement, whatever, all of it should come out into the open! Stan felt that in that way it would be the true test - to see who would prevail once they were armed with full knowledge of all the top opponents' strengths and weaknesses."

"And don't tell me all these strategic gems are going to be in your book?"

"You guessed it! Stan believed it'll become a golden era for women's tennis. He took the view that the game will scale new heights!"

"But please tell me that, as yet, Holly, Natalie, Jacalyn and Angela know nothing about this. You need to really take advice on whether this makes proper sense."

"Too late," parried Javea. "I've already decided to tell all four of them about what I am going to do. And I will tell them, over the next few weeks. You watch - this sport is about to get seriously spicy!"

Suddenly Javea was gone and Terry was alone. He signed for Javea's Perrier and mulled over what he now knew about the murky waters of tennis stardom. He worried for Javea because the guy seemed so insistent and oddly vulnerable. But then Terry remembered Javea's millions and his concern ebbed away rather quickly after that.

Traversing the atrium, returning slowly to the hotel lift, Terry tried to assimilate all that he had just heard. Javea must be mad! He planned to bring every festering sore into the public domain. His apparent rationale was to rid the game of unpleasant influences and herald a new dawn of scintillating competition. But would that really happen? Wouldn't Javea's own game falter? How would the individuals affected by Javea's revelations choose to react?

Terry pondered, too, on Javea's somewhat ambivalent response whenever Holly's name came into the conversation. Was he faithful to her? What would she do if he wasn't? And how on earth would Holly, as world No 1, treat her boyfriend once he published details of her tactical frailties in a book?

Perhaps Javea had been right. Certainly tennis looked as if it was heading for a seriously spicy time. But Javea's campaign of unadulterated honesty was sure to lead to some casualties and the game's glitterati would not thank him for airing their dirty laundry in public.

Once back in his large, air-conditioned room, Terry reflected on the evening's events and first conceded to himself that, for instance, he personally knew very little about Drew L Todd, other than he was a top agent who made a tremendous fortune by lining up endorsements for his star clients. What would Drew do if Javea broadcast something that threatened Drew's thriving money-making pleasure? Come to think of it, how would this Indian gangster, Karan, deal with allegations that he had tried to extort and bribe the tennis community? Surely, he would not be the type to turn a blind eye, especially as the shenanigans would show him in a desperate light, having effectively tried to buy the love of player Blanca Alessandra. As for the umpire, Smartson, he would be finished by Javea's story. For Blanca, the publicised notoriety could potentially push her over the edge.

Additionally, Terry could not see Holly Fleming, Angela de Jong, Jacalyn Jeanice or Natalie Sloane - or their respective entourages - taking kindly to publication of expert analysis on how to beat them. These girls were repeatedly battling it out for big monetary prizes, and with the titles came the high value sponsorships. Some, or one, of that group of four may feel particularly disadvantaged by the printing of their on-court weaknesses. As an example, Terry realised that it was an open secret on tour that Holly's parents disliked Javea. They would doubtless be livid at any act by Javea which could, even remotely, damage Holly's success.

The palm of Terry's right hand was clenched tight with tension. He consciously relaxed it, and found therein, crushed and folded up, the two pieces of paper handed to him earlier in the evening by Javea. Terry scrutinised the four household names and let out an involuntary, audible sigh.

So which one had an uncontrollable crush on Javea that threatened to get out of control? Which girl detested him due to some drama involving mixed doubles? Who was the drug taker? And how could any of the four be a calculating vixen, who seduced umpires in a bid to do anything and everything to make a career as productive as possible?

The reporter tried to temporarily let go of what he knew and the accompanying guesswork. He removed his clothes and hurriedly took to his bed, exhausted by the intrigue and speculation. He tried to will himself into a swift slumber. But he had the nagging feeling that all was not well in the world of Javea Jackson … and only time would give an answer.

Chapter 4

Although it was nearing the end of June, Holly Fleming perceived the British weather to still be harsh and unpredictable.

She felt that the dark clouds above aptly reflected her troubled mind on this Monday, Wimbledon's first day.

Holly felt in true turmoil. Wimbledon had always been her focus from as long back as she could remember. Her parents, Don and Trey, had been zealots determined that they would have one child, and one child only - and that their offspring would become a tennis legend.

There had been no deviation from the blueprint. When you are stuck out on a court for hours on end starting from the age of three, it was hardly surprising you excelled at the sport, thought Holly. And how could self-doubt occur when your goal-oriented parents had schooled you relentlessly in the art of mental toughness throughout your entire existence?

But having fought herself to No 1 in the world, Holly had come to realise that life didn't suddenly become a bowl of cherries. She still had to exercise and practise relentlessly. Hitting a ball when you were suffering from niggling injuries remained no joke. The rudeness and intrusion of the media were ever constant. The fans shouting out your first name as if they were your best buddy were harrowing and creepy. Furthermore, tripping from country to country to do mortal combat with your most fierce adversaries was a gut-wrenching pressure which she was only surviving by instinct and her physical aversion to losing.

In short, Holly felt that her life was becoming gradually more miserable, arduous and hollow. Pride was still a major catalyst, but her parents' unremitting presence meant no privacy.

If she had to describe her life, the words she would have used were "victim in a goldfish bowl". And yet Holly felt giddy and weightless beyond belief whenever she thought of one person - Javea.

And, in her mind, Javea was now inextricably linked with Wimbledon. The latter was by far her favourite Grand Slam; the Aussie Open venue lacked history and tradition, Roland Garros in Paris now felt small and over-crowded, whereas New York's Flushing Meadow simply lacked soul. It therefore seemed strange and perverse to Holly that she had triumphed at Melbourne, Roland Garros and at the US Open, but London SW19 was still to be conquered by her.

So her project was simple: win Wimbledon for Javea.

But now, with this tabloid exposé in the morning, Holly felt that life had played one big trick on her. It seemed Javea had cheated, and that ripped her equilibrium apart. Why now win Wimbledon at all, and why do anything whatsoever as an act of love for Javea? She wrestled with this conundrum, because earlier in the day her habitual positivity had bounced back, but as her meeting with Javea drew closer, she couldn't help but revisit her negativity.

And Holly also felt angry. She had a tournament to win and how dare Javea deflect her attentions from proper preparation. No doubt every press conference would now feature its fair share of fools exuding an unhealthy interest in the state of her coupledom with Javea. Why did she have to put up with all this? Simultaneously, her parents would jump on the bandwagon and resume their vocal criticism of her boyfriend. And how was she to defend him, now it seemed he had done the indefensible?

Honestly, at times like this she could kill Javea. Didn't he know how she had nightmares about facing the booming serve of Angela de Jong, a stuck-up princess who never acknowledged her? Didn't he comprehend the dread she suffered when precious

Jacalyn Jeanice stared right through her and clenched a fist with venom in their matches at Roland Garros? Couldn't Javea realise how hard it was to face Natalie Sloane on the slick grass of Centre Court with an entire British crowd clapping excitedly in response to any and every Holly error, whether it was forced or unforced?

It was a short walk from her temporary residence in Marryat Road to the cul-de-sac where Javea had taken a property for two weeks. At the bottom of Marryat Road, Holly joined Somerset Road and turned right. Behind the nondescript walls to her left lay the grounds of the All England Club where the Wimbledon tennis takes place. Not that you could see the walls! As ever, the fans queuing patiently for ground pass admittance obscured completely the boundary fences. The hordes stretched back for what seemed to be miles. Holly pulled down her baseball cap so her face was concealed.

The grounds of the event are roughly in a triangular shape, with the apex of the triangle snaking to a point at the southerly end of Somerset Road, just before the walker begins a hilly ascent into Wimbledon Village. In this fading part of the triangle - quite a distance from the drama of Centre Court - you will find the now omni-present corporate watering holes and "private marquees". Adjacent to them in the Wimbledon grounds habitually stood a sigh of yesteryear, a croquet lawn, but no-one mentions it much anymore. Holly's guess was that it was on the brink of destruction, if it hadn't gone already.

Yet for Holly it was still a thrill to be a competitor at the All England Club. Whenever she entered through the main gates at the club's official entrance - Gate 5 - she experienced a pang of excitement and anticipation. From an early age she remembered TV images of the public swarming around on the south concourse, which is where you are the minute you enter Gate 5. Though in those days, she thought to herself, the fans with ground pass tickets were content to watch the ivy clad scoreboards relaying point by point progress on Centre Court and Court No 1, at a time when the latter was situated exactly next door to the former. Now those same people would be highly impatient if the giant TV screen on the club's Aorangi Terrace was not available.

In 1996, after an autumnal Davis Cup tie won by Great Britain over Egypt - the last point of which was a double-fault - the "old" Court No 1 never saw any more action and it was demolished to make way for the Millennium Building, an impressive state-of-the-art structure which was now the competitors' complex. The truth was that, little by little, Wimbledon moved away from being an olde worlde garden party and became more and more expansive and spacious. Holly seemed to remember that the new Court No 1, and Courts 18 and 19 beside it, had only been made possible when the All England Club extended its borders by acquiring the neighbouring Aorangi Park.

Holly dragged herself back to her awful, immediate reality. At the foot of the hill leading to Wimbledon Village she crossed through the steady line of traffic. She passed a WPC who had been waylaid by two tracksuit-hooded fans, and walked into Javea's cul-de-sac named Rectory Orchard, which consisted of a handful of sizeable detached houses. Javea had the first such property on the right-hand side.

She rang the bell, grateful to have evaded any autograph hunters. She waited for Javea. After a pause of a few seconds she could make out - as a shadow in the glass of the door - his figure, imposing and raw-boned. Fleetingly, Javea reminded her of the star in so many teen films, and Scooby Doo ... what was his name?

"You really do look like Freddie Prinze Junior," she announced as blonde Javea appeared at the entrance. "I wonder whether he cheats on Sarah Michelle Gellar, or perhaps he's too scared of Buffy's magic powers!"

"Get inside," replied Javea, gruffly. "I was just doing some stuff on my laptop."

They each sat down warily on large black sofas, opposing each other. "So, what's the story, big champ Javea? What's it like with luscious Larissa?"

"Come on," responded Javea. "Don't tell me you are one of these absurd people who believe everything they read in the papers? Especially that particular tabloid?!"

"So what are you telling me? A girl just completely makes up a story and there's nothing in it whatsoever?"

"I just can't believe you don't trust me. I cannot believe I am with someone who wants to own me night and day. Holly, I am due on Centre Court in a few hours to begin the defence of my title. Do you know how much that means to me? And you're here just to divert my mind. What's the point of that? You call that love? Why can't you trust me?"

"I just can't bear to think of you involved with anyone else."

"Nothing's happening."

"Look, Javea, we both want to win Wimbledon. This isn't only about you. No doubt I'll be on Court No 1 tomorrow and I'll be caught in the lion's den against somebody hell bent on eliminating me. But I'll tell you something - I don't see any stories in the English newspapers saying that I've been having an affair with anyone other than the man I am supposed to be getting married to next month. I want to believe everything is OK. But I feel like I do everything in this relationship. I'm the one who always emails you, calls you, flies to where you are in the world. Do I get that sort of treatment in return? Relationships are not meant to be this one-sided. Tell me if you think I'm wrong. Look, I don't want to argue with you - I just want us to get back to how it was at the start, last year in Paris. When I was so happy ... when we were both so happy, right?"

Paris. The very word returned Holly to the best time of her life, 12 months before, in the French capital. Her parents had opted not to be there, the sun shone symbolically and her tennis - and very being - flourished as if released from a cage. On court, she could do no wrong; the ball appeared as big as a basketball and all seven of her bemused opponents walked away, defeated and shattered by the magic coming from her racket. Even the French aficionados had taken to her, with enthusiastic, repeated cries of "Allez Holleeee!" Providentially, her serenity was not even disrupted by the congested Roland Garros thoroughfare running from the main scoreboards all the way down to Court 1.

Better still, she kept bumping into the striking Javea - hitherto only a fellow pro tennis player (albeit one to whom she had in the past offered a financial helping hand) - at every turn. It was most unusual. At the hotel's reception desk, by its lifts, at breakfast on the 23rd floor, by the practice courts to the west of the Suzanne Lenglen stadium, inside the media centre …

So it seemed perfectly natural (they were both staying at the Sofitel Hotel on Rue Louis Armand) when she received a call in her room from Javea. As they each had a free day from any matches, he suggested casually that they could saunter over to the Eiffel Tower. Never before had they interacted away from tennis and on anything other than a professional, semi-distant basis. And when they reached the special sight, Javea was animated and gallant, telling her almost straight away that he had always found her absolutely gorgeous, and she was more than happy to repay the compliment. Buoyed by the mutual appreciation, the young couple soon found an excuse that springtime to interlock hands whilst admiring the French monument celebrating affairs of the heart.

The sickening siren of competition felt a long way away for Holly by the time they had made it to the second viewing level of the Eiffel Tower and together they absorbed the entire city beneath them. It was a tick in time, a passing portrait, that she never wanted to end, because nothing is better than being with someone who adores you and for whom you feel an overwhelming abundance of passion.

The rest of that priceless, idyllic, perfect day had passed by in a similarly lazy, blissful manner. From the Eiffel Tower, and its symbolic beauty, they trekked cheerily to the Arc de Triomphe. They climbed the 280 steps in an ecstatic way and enjoyed the panoramic vista, including the avenue des Champs-Elysees. The sun that afternoon remained fixed in Holly's mind in a euphoric haze. Even now, she felt a clenched sense of desire in her stomach whenever she looked at the inexpensive watch Javea had gifted her, a memento bought from a souvenir seller on place d'Etoile.

And now a voluptuous minx named Larissa LaDame had gone and eradicated this wonderful memory. Holly also felt that Javea was hiding something; his transparency seemed incomplete. She was sad that he was not making a bigger effort to reassure her. Not only did that hurt ... it was also ominous.

"How did you meet Larissa LaDame?"

"How do I know?" fired back Javea. "You know how it is, we meet so many people. A party for sponsors, autograph sessions, media commitments. No doubt she came up to me at some social thing and tried to scrape my acquaintance."

"So you resisted her?"

"Holly, it pays to be polite. If I was rude to some lady in public then the press would love it. I simply can't win. If I tell you I was pleasant to her, you'll call me flirtatious. If I ignored her completely, you'd say I was arrogant. What exactly do you want from me?"

"I want to know how this girl has persuaded a national newspaper that she had a non-platonic relationship with you. Two minutes of restrained conversation will not give her that opportunity."

"Oh, I don't know," said Javea. "Maybe she put her arm around me when I was talking to someone else so that a friend of hers could take mobile 'phone pictures to make it look like we were close. Maybe she has been following me on tour from one place to the next, so she could satisfy the paper that she knew where I always was."

"Let me get this straight. You admit you met her and talked to her, yes?"

"I'm saying probably that happened. But that doesn't make me a monster, does it? Surely I'm allowed to talk to people."

"So what did you talk about? Isn't it the weather that grabs the attention of you Brits?"

"Holly, don't tell me you've never had a star struck fan come up to you and lay on the compliments thick and heavy? Perhaps she told me that I was a great player, a credit to England, immensely talented - nothing unusual. Come on, even you get that stuff all the time!"

"The only difference is that I walk away as quickly as possible. It appears that you couldn't get enough of it."

"Yes, I talked. Was I flattered? Perhaps a little. Is the lady pretty? No doubt. But all it shows is that I am human, nothing else."

"Mmm. And don't they say that to err is to be human?"

"I didn't err to the extent that you are implying I erred. I'm certain that all her revelations will amount to this week is that she looked into my eyes, I looked into hers, I smiled when she made a joke, blah, blah, blah. The rest will be left to the sordid readers' imagination. Larissa clearly wants 15 minutes of fame. Unfortunately it is at my expense."

"So I haven't suffered at all, is that it?"

"I didn't say that."

"But that's what you think, isn't it? That I should just accept your blanket denial and get on with my life as if nothing has happened. I can't believe you!"

"You can't believe you shouldn't get on with your life or you don't believe I am innocent of what Larissa alleges? Which is it?"

"Javea! You're beginning to cross a line. You seem distracted when we're together. Distracted and bored. I've done nothing wrong, apart from love you always and entirely. Now there are rumours that you're seeing another girl. We're supposed to be getting married next month. You're not making me happy anymore, I'm telling you."

"So what do you want to do?"

"I want you to care. To convince me that you remain totally committed and in love with me. Is that too much to ask?"

"You see, it is only you, Holly, who is getting stressed about all of this. Life will go on and you've got to chill or else it'll kill you. If you're tense, you make me tense. I don't need this right now. I've got to win this tournament or I'll be lynched by a nation. It's like a ton of bricks of pressure on my shoulders. At this rate I'll be a break down in the first set before I've even found my feet out there today! Can't you see that now is not the time for this type of conversation?"

"I just feel that our life is not what it was. You were never like this at the beginning. You were the one who told me that I was your vitality, that you could never be without me, that we should get married! And that was just a few short months ago. Now what's going on, Javea, why do I feel that everything is so completely different for us now? If in fact there still is an 'us'."

"Well, do you think we should split up? At least - temporarily."

"You mean, it wouldn't worry you if we came to an end," voiced Holly, gently. "If all our promises to each other ultimately came to nought?"

"There'll always be a type of love between us, won't there?" asked Javea, his voice thick with tightness.

"And yet you're quite happy to so easily let go of me," ventured Holly. "After all we've been through; the dream couple."

"It's not like that," insisted Javea.

"But you do like someone else, right?" quizzed Holly. "There's someone who you think can give you more than I can."

"No," Javea responded, defensively.

"Jacalyn Jeanice? Is that it? Some French airhead is what you want, is it?"

"No, no, no," came Javea's riposte.

"But she's incessantly after you, always talking about you," stated Holly. "I can see it in her eyes that she's after you. Or is it one of my other enemies? Not Natalie Sloane - no, she's not your type, but I can see you showing a special interest in Angela de Jong! And I bet she wouldn't say no to you of all people!"

Javea sensed that Holly's anger was about to boil. He had long understood that in such circumstances it was best to keep silent until the hurricane blew itself out.

"You're worthless, Javea, and spineless. You want me to make the decision that we're through and you've tried to leave me with no choice by your being so meek and pathetic. How you ever won Wimbledon is a mystery to me! You're nothing, absolutely nothing!"

"And you keep making my life a misery, so what am I supposed to do?"

"I thought we were forever, Javea, forever!! What has Larissa got that I haven't? What haven't I given you? You've taken everything from me - everything! Remember how I helped fund your career a few years back when you were still struggling to make ends meet and I was already a world-beater! We weren't even a couple back then. And this is how you repay me!"

"Oh, so you tried to buy me, is that it?" stormed Javea. "I was poor so you bought me and now I'm supposed to be perpetually grateful and remain in my box!"

Holly regarded Javea as if he was the devil. He thought she would slap him. But the consummate discipline of the women's world No 1 prevailed, and she audibly took a very deep breath to compose herself.

"I should never have got involved with you, Javea. You have no ethics and you don't deserve someone as very special as me. My parents were right - I can, and will, do better. You're just a flash in the pan, a one hit wonder - and you'll never win anything again. So, here, have a parting gift." She opened the expensive shoulder bag which she had brought with her. Sniffing slightly, she reached inside it. "A pot of beloved marmalade for your beloved pre-match meal! Good luck out there - if you've got the mettle to make it. Sorry that I forgot the white toast to go with it!" The last words were literally hurled at Javea as Holly ran out of the house.

Holly narrowly avoided running into the back of the WPC at the end of the road (who was again being pestered by tennis followers) and she sprinted past onlookers all the way back to Marryat Road.

In contrast, in his dwelling, sitting alone, Javea found reason to be very pleased with himself.

Chapter 5

To many pundits, the first 24 hours of the Wimbledon fortnight are perhaps the most exciting. You don't see the top players in action against each other, but nothing can beat the air imbued with the sense of edginess on the "first Monday".

One hundred and twenty-eight men, one hundred and twenty-eight women. All, on paper when you read the names in the draw, with an equal chance of winning their respective tournaments.

And no-one can tell exactly what's going to happen. Terry Proudley thought back, with journalistic nostalgia, to the first Wimbledon he could properly recall, that of 1978. He came back from school on the first Monday afternoon and there on TV was the Swedish champion Bjorn Borg, struggling for his life on the Centre Court in the first round against an American unknown, Victor Amaya.

At the time the significant crux of the match had been lost on young Terry. He didn't even know what a service break was! But for the audience who witnessed it, Borg versus Amaya was an incredible, epic five set journey. Borg, the Nordic hero, and master of Wimbledon the two previous years, fell behind two sets to one, and was even a point away from going 1-4 down in the fourth set! But the Viking genius somehow scraped out of trouble and eventually came through by the eccentric scoreline of 8-9, 6-1, 1-6, 6-3, 6-3. And he went on to capture the 1978 Wimbledon, whipping arch-rival Jimmy Connors easily in the final.

The following year the legend from Stockholm again found the initial rounds unimaginably tough, causing mass panic amongst his multitude of fans. Once again he lost the first set on the first Monday on Centre Court, before overcoming Tom Gorman, an economics graduate from Seattle, 3-6, 6-4, 7-5, 6-1. But that was a mere prelude to the disaster that nearly befell him in the second round on the "old" Court No 1 against the Indian stylist, Vijay Amritraj.

The idol from Madras led by two sets to one and nearly bounced Borg out in the tense fourth set tie-breaker. But the Swede survived and won Wimbledon '79 ... and Wimbledon '80. In the latter tournament it was his nemesis John McEnroe who nearly sank early in the competition, only overcoming an Aussie rank outsider called Terry Rocavert on an outer court, No 3, in five sets in the second round.

Even after the 1980s and the days of five-times Wimbledon champion Borg, problems still exist early in the event for the established stars. Holly could recall her heroine Steffi Graf slithering to defeat in the first round in 1994 to San Diego-born Lori McNeil. Holly felt certain that the events which had just occurred at Javea's place would surely mean that she, too, collapsed at the formative stages of this Wimbledon. What had happened there at Javea's had been awful - and now she could not turn the clock back. If only he hadn't been so quick to accept the relationship was over! That was when she had become really mad. But how could he have been so willing to see her walk out of his life? Whom was better suited for Javea than herself? And now everything was all over, Holly mused. There was no turning back and she would have to face the music. One thing was for sure: Holly couldn't cope with practice today. She fell into bed and felt the ripples of sadness and sorrow envelop her.

Terry Proudley was himself taken aback not to find someone else on a practice court. At 10am, it was customary to notice Javea Jackson - a man of great ritual - hitting some warm-up points with one of his fellow pros. But Terry could not locate Javea at the competitors' practice courts near the Aorangi Pavilion. So the reporter, as pleased as ever to be inside the All England Club grounds, set off past the Church Road side of Court No 1, heading past various kiosks towards courts 14-17 inclusive.

But still there was no sign of Javea, who was due on Centre Court in just three hours. The masses were beginning to congregate inside the tournament site, with play due to start on the outer courts at midday.

Terry pushed on, past the bandstand to his left, through the tea lawn, and then he turned right onto the south concourse. He quickly worked his way along the backs of courts 5, 4 and 3, and walked briskly inside the tunnel beneath the stands of courts 2 and 3.

He peered onto the turf of Court No 2 from the vantage point inside the tunnel, but still couldn't see Javea. He rushed onwards to check, in turn, courts 6-10 inclusive. Although other competitors were warming up, including Angela de Jong and Jacalyn Jeanice with their respective male hitting partners, Javea was absent. Terry next tried at the remaining courts at the south end of the grounds, but again the players practising did not include Javea.

Terry returned to the press centre via the Somerset Road parameters of the All England Club. He looked fondly at Court No 6, where he had first glimpsed John McEnroe, who had been enthralling packed crowds in a doubles match played on the opening Friday of the 1979 Championships.

But even that happy memory was now tinged with a pang of concern about Javea. Since their chat in Dubai in March, Terry had followed Javea's progress far more closely, and was deeply disappointed when Jackson bowed out a month earlier, in May, in the semi-finals of the red clay Grand Slam, the French Open.

Despite the sometimes brusque character of Javea, the fact was that Terry felt very comfortable with what seemed the direct, no nonsense approach of Jackson.

And then Terry remembered - he had forgotten to check Courts 18 and 19! They were situated to the west side of the new Court No 1 and, even though they had now been there a few years, Terry was apt to still forget them! So, feeling boosted, Terry passed Gate 13, albeit still a tad sad that the beautiful lodge cottage that once stood there, admittedly somewhat incongruously, had disappeared when the Millennium Building arose. But he waved aside that thought and walked up the stairs of St Mary's Walk, past the hallowed Centre Court to his right. At least the life of the lodge had been over 80 years, as it had been erected in about 1922.

Terry almost cavorted past the broadcast centre in his desire to see the reassuring presence of Javea on court. Yet as he went up the slope between Courts 18 and 19, he found that neither court boasted the Wimbledon men's champion. So where the hell was Javea?

Terry retraced his steps and walked back to his computer in the press centre. Clearly, there would be some innocent explanation. And, miracle of miracles, when Terry switched on his email facility, he noticed that the very last one was from Javea Jackson himself!

Terry had never received an email from Javea, but he knew that your email id was readily accessible when you worked on a national paper. Javea's communication was entitled "Hi ya, Terry!", and read as follows:

"Yo man, howz everything?

I know, I know, you don't expect to hear from me, but I like you, man, and think I get on with you. But this email is what the lawyers call without prejudice, and I respect the fact that you'll respect my privacy!!

I wanted to clear something up about Holly, and to do so with someone who can't see me, but who can understand me. The truth is that I think some girl, yes one Larissa LaDame, is out to extort money from me by threatening me with intimate stories sold to the trash papers.

I need you to know that they are not true, Terry. I have NOT physically cheated on Holly. So you make sure that in the press you do what you can to maintain my good rep, yeah? I'm really sorry I gave you nothing juicy in Dubai, but I like to play my cards close to my chest. As I'm apparently a star, many people are out to get me now. Such as Larissa. The way people like her work is that they expect you to pay to maintain their silence, and each time you resist a money demand, they get something printed about you and say the price will be higher next time to avoid more serious disclosures.

Yes, I've seen Larissa at events from time to time, but just in a public place and to say hello to. To be honest, I always say hello and smile a lot when I see a female's pretty face. Call it my weakness, whatever. But to put it another way, Terry, this story of Larissa's is not one that can hurt me at all. Ahah! Now you're not understanding, right? Well, life's gotta be exciting and I'm making yours more exciting, yes? Because you can try to work out what's happening!! So now we both have something to aim for this Wimbledon: me, my second title. You, what the hell Javea is going on about?!! Together with safeguarding my good reputation, remember.

So wish me luck, Terry, out there on court today with the expectations of the country on my back. You've gotta admire Henman, right? How did he cope all those years??!!?? I guess, because like me, he thrived on the attention, if the truth be told. What makes us different is that we have nerves of steel. We can ignore what the scoreboard says and play each point with true concentration, in its own compartment. We never admit defeat. We will battle to the end however hopelessly lost the cause looks. We have every faith in our shots and can hit them splendidly even in our sleep. We find nothing tiring or remotely boring about practising up to six hours a day, in the boiling heat if necessary, and then doing weights and gym work! Yup, we are nutters all right - but happy nutters determined to get ourselves as close to tennis perfection as possible.

Anyways, that's enough from me. Enjoy Wimbledon. Stay in touch. Have a great one.

Yours,

Javea."

Terry was delighted to receive a personal email from the tennis marvel for whom all his peers were clamouring. It was a good portent for the future. If Terry could get regular information and snippets of news from Javea, it could only enhance Terry's career prospects and general profile in the game. Terry was also tranquillised by Javea's email. Clearly, the guy was in a jovial mood and was blatantly without a care in the world. How else could you explain Javea's taking time off from practice on the first day of the Championships in order to spread a bit of cheer in Terry's direction?

Holly would obviously be gratified, thought Terry, when she came to realise that Larissa LaDame was nothing more than an evil troublemaker, trying by dishonesty to break up a couple on the verge of matrimony. Terry was impressed by the way in which Javea was able to sweep to one side such baseless slander. There was no desire by Javea to seek recourse from the courts, even though he could no doubt make a hefty sum in damages if he did so.

Chapter 6

Terry was still somewhat blissful as he made his way into his allotted seat in the Centre Court press stands at about 12.55pm. He had printed off the email, put it in his back pocket, lunched happily and then wandered around the various outside courts, drinking in the pleasure of the opening Wimbledon skirmishes.

It was hard for him not to feel a little patriotic as he now gazed down at the immaculate grass and reflected on the fact that his compatriot Javea Jackson had earned the right to commence Wimbledon's Centre Court clashes this year by bagging the title crown 12 months earlier.

Of course, there had been a prodigious surge in tennis' popularity in the country as a consequence of that accomplishment. Players of all ages were swarming onto the park courts every day of the week, inspired by Jackson's stupendous feat.

Play was due to begin on Centre Court, by recent tradition, "at 1pm precisely". That was when Javea was required to walk out in front of 14,000 fans and one billion world-wide television viewers, flanked by his unseeded opponent.

Only, it didn't happen. For the first time - ever. The stadium was full to capacity, all present were ready to give a roar of greeting to their hero. But the minutes ticked by and the players did not appear.

By 1.20, Terry was anxious and the hoi polloi began an impatient slow hand clap to signify their displeasure. Was Javea or his opponent ill, wondered Terry? That must be it. In which case, one of the guys would soon be claiming a walkover and, sensationally, Centre Court would be deprived of watching the reigning champion!

Terry's intuition turned out to be incorrect. Down on court he saw the All England Club chairman shuffling slowly towards the empty umpire's chair. The distinguished personage took to the high chair and the congregation silenced itself immediately to catch the announcement. "Ladies and Gentlemen," he intoned without emotion, "the scheduled first match on the Centre Court Order of Play has regrettably had to be cancelled and we can give no further news in this respect at the current time. We greatly appreciate your forbearance. There will be an interval of an hour, or more - we are not sure yet - and then the Ladies Singles will continue, and playing on Centre Court will be Miss Jacalyn Jeanice of France versus Miss Roxanne Miller of Great Britain."

The throng booed and howled in displeasure. Terry was instantly out of his seat and rushing to the press conference room. This time he trusted his instinct that his collective colleagues would be calling determinedly for a full briefing from both the chairman and the tournament referee. Once inside the media centre he heard Sue Barker, the BBC TV anchorwoman, looking tense into her camera, saying: "Well, we'll of course bring you more news as soon as we have it, but all we can say for now is that this is a most bizarre and unorthodox beginning to the Championships. John Lloyd, what do you make of all this?"

Terry didn't hear the reply from the Englishman who had been the Australian Open runner-up in 1977. When he reached the press conference, he had to content himself with standing at the back of the crammed room. Sure enough, he saw the chairman and tournament referee sitting at the front, their twin faces melting second by second into increasing sweat which was induced by the bright spotlights beaming down on them.

"Ladies and Gentlemen," began the chairman gravely, "this is a media announcement in respect of which there exists a publication embargo until 3pm this afternoon. The committee of management of these Championships deeply regrets having to inform you that the reigning men's Champion and world No 1, Mr Javea Jackson, was found dead a couple of hours ago at his rented accommodation close to the tournament grounds. This will be an immense shock to all of you gathered here, and we express our heartfelt and profuse sorrow to everybody who knew and loved him."

Before the tumult of press noise erupted, the referee just had time to add: "The men's Championship will now be curtailed this year as a mark of utmost deference to Mr Jackson."

Chapter 7

By the time of London's rush hour, the news of Jackson's appalling demise was plastered on the billboards outside every tube station. Each placard read simply: "JAVEA JACKSON DEAD".

Terry was not pleased that the Evening Echo provocatively entitled his front page piece "WAS IT SUICIDE?" Written under vast time pressure, and clearly showing the strains of the writer's own emotion, the article proclaimed:

"DEFENDING WIMBLEDON TENNIS CHAMPION, British hero Javea Jackson, was found dead earlier today at his rented house in Rectory Orchard, Wimbledon.

The horrific news was broken to shocked journalists at about 1.30pm this afternoon, at an impromptu press conference held at the All England Club.

There were gasps of shock and some distraught reporters started weeping as club officials disclosed the unbelievable news.

Star Javea was of course due to open the Centre Court programme at 1pm precisely today because this honour goes every year to the defending male Champion.

But the 18 year-old did not come into view at 1 o'clock and the devotees were slow handclapping their disappointment within 20 minutes of his no-show. The same action-starved fans will now have to come to terms with a far greater and all-encompassing loss.

At the time it was thought that he might be injured - but the truth has turned out to be far worse than anything else that could have been countenanced.

Quite simply, the nation has inexplicably lost one of its favourite sons and the sport will never be the same ever again. It would be a fitting tribute if the club is decked out next year entirely in black, rather than its regular mauve and green. The sense of bereavement is that all pervading.

Already Wimbledon authorities have conveyed their 'immense shock and heartfelt sorrow'. And, quite rightly, the men's singles event has immediately been cancelled this year as a mark of respect to Javea. I understand that the majority of the men's stars privately support this decision, probably because they also want time to mourn one of the greats of tennis.

Javea's fiancée, the American ladies World No 1 Holly Fleming, was unavailable for comment. Florida's finest export, 21, is apparently hiding her grief at her own accommodation just a stone's throw from Centre Court - where we had hoped to applaud another Jackson victory today.

The tournament was shrouded in confusion once Javea's death was divulged to the press and it is not even clear if Holly Fleming will play on through the pain of her own very private deprivation and misfortune. The starlet was due to marry Jackson next month. Only time will tell how she manages and reacts to this tragedy.

Astonishingly, on the eve of Wimbledon, Jackson sensationally confided in me: 'None of us know how long we have got in the game.' Now his words stand poignant and pointed - as well as prophetic.

And I can reveal that the 18 year-old celebrity in fact wrote me a personal email this morning, which we now know was just before his wholly unexpected death. In the email, Jackson told me: 'Enjoy Wimbledon ... have a great one.'

There was no reason to believe that Jackson was unhappy in his life. After all, he has become a world-wide superstar with endorsements to match. Unbelievably, he made all his own commercial deals after terminating the services of top tennis agent, New Yorker Drew L Todd. In that way Jackson was a throwback to a more innocent era when players seized their titles without the backing of a huge travelling entourage.

He had also found love in the form of the awesome player Holly Fleming.

The irony is that the Briton had attained all this fame and fortune after escaping from humble and austere childhood days. An orphan by nine, he dedicated himself to tennis, doing what he saw as a possible passport to inner peace. And yet today that zestful existence has been curtailed without any reason.

A police press conference is anticipated later today to update us on the investigation. Until then it would be wrong and inappropriate to speculate on the cause or nature of the death.

The top stars of tennis are 'A' listers at any party and therefore not immune from the interests of mad men and stalkers.

Former pros Bjorn Borg and John McEnroe both have played on court despite being the subject of death threats - Borg in the US Open final of 1981 and McEnroe at Wimbledon '89. In that event, McEnroe fought gamely to the semi-finals despite almost daily anonymous telephone calls to newspapers and to the All England Club, proclaiming that he would be shot if he went out in front of the people. He competed that year flanked at all times by a horde of security guards - but in modern times, especially after the appalling stabbing of Monica Seles in 1993, security at tennis has become ever more intense.

Also, at a minor professional tournament at West Hampstead's Cumberland Club in 1983, gunfire stopped play. It turned out to be a prankster firing blanks from a nearby apartment block.

But today we mourn an inspirational figure who stood at the beginning of a brilliant career. Experts believe that he would certainly have matched legend Fred Perry's three Wimbledon titles and may well have gone on to surpass Pete Sampras' haul of seven. Now we will never know - and we won't see the likes of Javea Jackson on Centre Court again.

It is too early to say how this will affect the rest of the Wimbledon fortnight. Most men players are likely to jet out of England over the next couple of days, leaving the Championships to be an exclusively female affair. Whether the ladies can bring any resemblance or hint of a smile back to this meeting is hard to tell. It will be very difficult for the likes of Holly Fleming, Angela de Jong, Jacalyn Jeanice and our own Natalie Sloane to compensate for today's ghastly turn of events.

It will be an almost ghostly affair late afternoon today when Warwickshire's wild card entrant Roxanne Miller takes on No 3 seed Jeanice from Paris. For most of us, the apparition of Javea Jackson will cast an ominous shadow over the entire surroundings."

And Terry Proudley would be the first to admit that tears streaked his own distressed face as soon as Javea's death was known to him. It simply made no sense for such a young and vibrant life to be destroyed so early. Clearly, the teenager hadn't been anticipating his death, reflected Terry. The email showed that Javea Jackson was in good spirits and determined to win Wimbledon again. Unless he hadn't written it himself, but that was most unlikely. Terry shivered. Conspiracy stories frightened him. And yet there had been something - just one thing - a little odd about Javea's communication. That phrase *"this story of Larissa's is not one that can hurt me ... "* What on earth had he meant by that? Surely Javea could see that any story linking him with an untalented good-time girl was bad for his image? Either Javea had loved her, or he had simply been too trusting to know a temptress when he met one. Terry wondered what the truth could possibly be.

Chapter 8

Larissa LaDame was in the environs of Wimbledon at the time Javea had died. No-one quite knew what her exact movements had been, because she was a secretive girl who found that she benefited when her whereabouts were a mystery.

She had been dropped immediately by one tabloid as a result of Jackson's death, but in any event still had an earlier deal with another to be a "roving reporter" during the tournament, even though she had absolutely no journalistic qualifications. The cynical motivation for her appointment was that it was hoped she would charm the players and watching celebrities into indiscreet conversation or behaviour. And this malicious intent was hidden behind the disingenuous argument that she was well placed, because of her Javea connection, to capture the essence of Wimbledon with a "social diary" column.

Larissa knew that Javea's death could make her a lot of money. After all, he was a national icon and she was willing to say how she spent those last months making him happier than Holly Fleming ever did. That would be publishing dynamite. Obviously the press would want to be respectful and dignified for a suitable period of time, but after that had gone, Larissa reckoned that almost certainly a lucrative, full blown book offer would definitely come her way. In fact, Javea's demise could only prove fortunate for her.

As news of the day's events passed like wildfire through the All England Club grounds, the vast majority of the spectators felt that it would be somehow inappropriate to watch tennis and there was, as a result, a mass exodus via all the gates.

Women's matches were the only ones in progress in this deserted habitat, and Terry, having filed his story, was dawdling aimlessly when he noticed Larissa entering the Cafe Pergola, next to the Fred Perry statue. Intrigued, having matched her insouciant, ripe appearance with the morning's newspaper photo, he ran over swiftly, introduced himself and soon they jointly decided to order a bottle of champagne to dull the acute situation and mutual awkwardness.

"How well do you know Javea ... did you know him?" began Terry, once they had sat down.

The hard-faced girl stared at her inquisitor. "I knew him all right. He was a real sweetie. It's too bad that a great guy has left us all behind."

"It doesn't sound that he mattered too much to you."

"I'm a realist, that's all. We all of us have to go some time. Too bad he went today. But what can I do about it?"

"What do you think the police will reveal at tonight's press conference?"

"How should I know? Your guess is as good as mine. Perhaps he had some congenital heart defect, and that was that."

"Possibly. But Javea, being a star athlete, has probably had more health and fitness check-ups than most of us would have in 100 lifetimes. So I don't believe your theory is very likely, do you?"

Larissa looked at Terry, who in turn eyed her enticing jet-black shoulder length hair. They broke the moment by each taking a sip of champagne. He sensed that he wanted to blame someone for today's disaster, and wide-eyed, smirking Larissa was the one directly in his line of fire.

"Maybe people didn't like him much," offered Larissa.

"But who?"

"I dunno; his girlfriend, perhaps. I guess she must have hated me for stealing Jav away from her."

"So why didn't she kill you instead? Pardon my asking, but wouldn't that have been more logical?"

"Murderers aren't logical, are they," replied Larissa, proud of her sound reasoning. "I mean, if you're in your right mind, you don't go killing anyone, do you?"

"What about provocation, then?" responded Terry. "Wouldn't it be true that your running to the media would have caused severe stress to Holly Fleming?"

"Listen," said Larissa. "If a guy's worth having - if you think that - then you gotta realise others may want him too, right. So there's no property in a man, believe me. They are all out there to be won, if you've got the game for it. Let's just say that Holly finished as runner-up to me!"

"That's absurdly tasteless, today of all days," scolded Terry. "The man has just died and all you can think about is whether you were the 'winner' against Holly, who no doubt is grieving terribly."

LaDame, still only a teenager, but so self-composed, poured herself another glass of champagne. "That's all life is about, Terry. Winners and losers. And all that really matters is winning the hottest guy and living the richest life with him. So I was successful, I think. And I can sell my story cos I was with a living legend ... only he's not living now, but that only makes my story all the more valuable. I mourn his death, really I do, but I will not be overly sentimental. He was just one guy, and life becomes normal again, it always does."

Terry mellowed a little. She was young, callow and tactless. Selfish, too. But there was a grain of truth in what this fortune-seeker said. Javea would want life to go on. He would have merely chuckled at the men's event being cancelled in his honour, but he would have had a veritable twinkle in his eye knowing that he had inadvertently managed to secure for women's tennis an exclusive worldwide TV audience.

"So, at least on some level, you loved him?" Terry asked Larissa.

"Oh, no, not really," shot back the girl. "He looked great, that's all. Blond and wiry. Muscular as well. But it was never love - I'm too young for that!"

"Can't love strike at any age?" questioned Terry.

"I'm not sure love exists - or fidelity," said Larissa. "And if you ask me, Jav was probably murdered, cos I don't think he had a dodgy heart, either."

Having dropped that bombshell on him, Terry was left with no further option to interrogate Larissa LaDame. The youngster simply bolted down some more champagne, thanked him abundantly, said she'd "gotta run" and disappeared in a rush. Terry was left to consider her words. He believed LaDame was a nasty piece of work, perhaps simply following orders from unsavoury men who were probably controlling her for their own financial ends. He shuddered unhappily. Looking at his watch, he could tell the police press conference would soon be in progress. He paid for the champagne and left Cafe Pergola promptly, not wanting to miss any information relating to the official enquiry.

The latter news from the police, when it came out that evening, was as bad as Terry anticipated it could have been. It was suspected that Javea Jackson had been the subject of murder by a person or persons unknown. No-one had yet been apprehended in this regard. The motive for his killing was as yet unfathomable. There was no sign of a break-in at his property. It was highly likely the culprit or culprits had been known to Javea. The police had received no prior threats on Javea's life. The murder had taken place by poisoning. When pressed, the police admitted in the news conference that, specifically, they had found poisoned marmalade at the residence. The source of poison was believed to be a type of rat poison. Yes, security had, in response, been stepped up for the female stars of Wimbledon, although no tangible threats had been received against any of them.

Finally, asked by Terry Proudley if anyone in particular would be questioned, the police spokesman replied amazingly, "We will presumably be starting with you, Mr Proudley."

Chapter 9

The indirect accusation made against him by a chief inspector in front of a room of people made Terry somewhat dejected, to say the least. No doubt the confession in his earlier, news-breaking article - that Javea had sent him an email on the fateful day itself - was enough to arouse some level of official suspicion.

Terry felt his nerves rising. He had to simply play it cool and trust that everything would blow over. So he left the media centre behind and took off with his laptop to find somewhere quiet to write. The Evening Echo had no further editions that day, but he still had to file something for the following day's first edition. In the end, Terry retreated to the cafe by Court 11 and, in this relatively calm backwater, he typed out a leaden and uninspired update about the police news conference.

The stressed-out hack couldn't think of any way to start his story, but eventually decided that the theme of the piece would be that this had been the darkest day at Wimbledon since October 1940 when German bombs attacked the place and caused the destruction of part of the Centre Court roof and 1,200 of its seats.

And again, after concluding the factual crux of his feature, Terry decided to wax lyrical. He finished emotively:

"…But Wimbledon, and life, will go on. It has to. So much has happened to so many generations all over the globe since this glorious summer event began way back in 1877. The Championships moved from its original nearby home, Worple Road, in 1922 to its current Church Road location, where it was opened by King George V. At the time no-one knew if it would be successful, but so many people were positive and now the word 'Wimbledon' is known the world over. Many of us have grown up through our own many life events whilst keeping our annual attendance at this tournament. In an ever-changing environment, Wimbledon is a reassuring, immovable yearly treat that will never decline or disappear."

And with that, Terry Proudley was officially off work for the day. He surveyed the darkening skies ahead and noted that the matches were almost over; only one or two lone battles continued on some of the outside courts. Earlier, he had heard on the grapevine, from some fans, that a game he had not watched, Jacalyn Jeanice against Roxanne Miller, had predictably enough been won by the nubile Parisien.

Terry was still troubled by his date the next day with the police as he resolved to leave the grounds. There was nowhere for him to go at this time of night except back to his own home, a small studio flat about 15 minutes walk away, next to Wimbledon Common. Besides, it was getting chilly now and his body ached from the day's trauma. He yearned for a long, very hot bath to soothe the tension away, even if it would only give a transient respite.

The journalist made his way along the deserted narrow path running eastwards from Court 11 in the direction of the club's distinctive water tower covered in the characteristic ivy, a fortuitous landmark remnant that had been there since 1922. What had the old cottage lodge by Gate 13 done to die, thought Terry, whilst the water tower over here continued to survive? (In fact, Terry may have been hallucinating, because the water tower was actually demolished after Wimbledon 2007!) And what had Javea done to expire on this baffling day? And why did he, Terry Proudley, have to be the first guy to be called in for questioning?

His anxiety gnawed away at him as he moved away from the Court 13 stands and walked alongside, on his left, initially court 10, and then court 5. He briefly recalled his meeting with Larissa LaDame when he saw Cafe Pergola to his right, but chiefly he was bound up in his own cares when he found himself back on the main, south concourse. He couldn't help but think about all those previous times he had enjoyed passing through the black, wrought-iron Doherty Memorial gates at the club's main entrance, Gate 5, which ultimately in early 2006 had been relocated to the Somerset Road end of the grounds. As any ardent student of tennis knew, the gates had been donated to the All England authorities in 1931 by the Reverend William Doherty, as a memorial to his younger brothers, Laurie and Reggie, who won between them nine Wimbledons at the turn of the 20th century.

Terry was just moving through Gate 5 when a come-hither but somewhat cloying female voice behind him declared: "Mr Proudley, I think we should talk, don't you?"

He turned round to face a 5ft tall WPC. The police, he lamented inwardly, and at this hour. But the face he was looking down at could only be described, undeniably, as compelling. Either she was Italian or perhaps an Indian of light complexion; he wasn't that good on nationalities. The all-white Hollywood smile came at him in a flirtatious, confident and cute manner. Big brown eyes sparkled in a way that induced a reflex dream-like condition. He didn't mind her uniform, either.

"Pleased to meet you," beamed the WPC, disarmingly.

"Likewise, and you," grinned Terry, truthfully.

"Is there somewhere we can talk?" asked the WPC. "I'm WPC Verita Sassi, by the way."

"And you look sassy, believe me," came Terry's gauche rejoinder.

The young woman laughed. People tried to push past them at the gate. "Come on," she urged, "how about a spot of dinner in the village up the hill? I presume you know it."

"Yes, I live here. I mean nearby," replied Terry, as they together moved out of the All England Club, and to their right.

"I think I can save you some pain," said WPC Sassi in a sexy whisper, her breath suddenly at his ear. "I'm off duty right now and yet I'm assigned - albeit with many others - to the Jav killing, so I could log a report tomorrow of what you've told me."

They continued incisively on their way past Rectory Orchard. The road was sealed off and they exchanged nervous glances, knowing that murder had occurred there just a few hours earlier.

"It's creepy," admitted the policewoman. "Do y'know I was on duty today, guarding this entrance to Rectory Orchard. It should be easy, right? A cul-de-sac. But somehow right behind me this legend Javea Jackson was dying, and I knew nothing about it."

"Well, he was poisoned," ventured Terry. "I don't see how we'll ever know who administered it."

"So you have no belief in us," sighed Sassi, turning to look deep into Terry's eyes. "That's so sad," she added wistfully.

"Well, somehow I'm beginning to feel less sad," came the coded response.

"That's good. So tell me tonight what that email is all about and I'll probably be able to get a cancellation of your interview tomorrow."

"How exactly do I say your name again?" asked Terry inquisitively, freshened by the words he heard.

"It's WPC Verita Sassi. If you want background, I'm 20 years old, have always been determined to work in the police force, and, yes, my parents are Italian but I have spent my entire life in England. This investigation will give me an excellent chance to show my prowess and willingness to work hard. And I think my superiors will be pleased that I hunted you down tonight, rather than wait until tomorrow - when you might have forgotten something important. I take it I can get a look now at that email Jav sent you today?"

"Absolutely. I shall aim to please."

"Make sure that you do, because I'm counting on it."

The rest of their advance towards the Bayee Village Chinese restaurant in Wimbledon Village seemed to Terry captivating and extremely amiable, even though it was simply a conversation about who might possibly win the women's singles. The fact that his new companion also told him he was the most handsome journalist she'd seen at the tournament didn't hurt, either.

Chapter 10

The presence of a very pretty uniformed female police constable ruffled no feathers at the Bayee Village. The staff were all far too professional and discreet to let anything bother them. After all, they had a knack of indulging distinguished customers and were even well equipped to service every showbiz whim, as proven by signed photos on the walls from tennis stars such as Andre Agassi and Martina Navratilova.

The lighting was tasteful: dim but enchanting. Terry and WPC Sassi were lucky enough to be granted a discreet corner table for two. Then Terry, uncomfortable with any silence, raised a query. "So, apart from my being as handsome as you are beautiful, what makes the police so interested in me?"

"You know how it is, Terry. You travel the world to all these tournaments and so have seen a lot more of Jav than we ever did. Nearest I ever got to him was watching him on telly. We all know that he was a troubled orphan who single-mindedly set his sights on tennis glory, and we all know that he was ready to marry this player Holly Fleming from the States. But what else do we really know? He liked marmalade with white toast before his matches?! Great! Where does that truly take us?"

"He never spent much time with me, I am afraid," replied Terry with caution. "But I can show you his email of today." He reached to his pocket for the copy, but was interrupted by the waiter passing them the menus.

"Thank you," said Terry, handing one to the WPC.

"Some drinks?" enquired the waiter.

Terry looked at the policewoman. "I find that double vodka and diet coke usually does it for me," came the sing-song reply, accompanied by a beguiling smile aimed directly at the server.

"In which case, we will have two of those," announced Terry, eager to reassert his stamp on proceedings. "And, unless my companion disagrees, please bring us sweet and sour prawns and vegetable chow mein," he added.

"His companion does not disagree," said WPC Sassi in a throaty voice, directing her gaze at the waiter. "Though some prawn crackers in advance would not go amiss."

The lady has a healthy appetite, noted Terry, as the waiter walked away from their table. Fragile, petite, gorgeous - but with a healthy appetite. What a wonderful combination!

She could see he was deep in thought - doubtless about her - and decided to unsettle him. "So, now we've ordered, can we get on with police business?" she asked sharply.

"Absolutely," relented Terry. "Here's his email." He handed it over to her and began speaking whilst she started reading it. "It says very little, in actual fact. Javea admits that in our earlier conversation, in Dubai, he had said nothing of significance, and added that he was looking forward to trying to win Wimbledon again, despite all the pressure, of course."

"What's all this about Larissa LaDame?" interjected WPC Sassi, reading quickly. "You've omitted to comment upon this portion of the text that says he cannot be hurt by Larissa's revelations and that this leaves something for you to work out. Well, have you? Have you worked it out, Mr Proudley?"

The sudden arrival at that point of the vodkas and prawn crackers bought Terry a little time to frame his reply. "I don't really know," he began. "But I think Javea simply meant that no publicity was bad publicity and therefore Larissa was free to continue to sell her supposedly true stories about him to whomever would be silly enough to pay her."

"I don't agree," shot back WPC Sassi, her sexy brown eyes narrowing a little. She snapped a prawn cracker in her mouth. "Javea Jackson basically asks you in the email to safeguard his good reputation. So what exactly is going on? Had he earlier threatened you in some way, is that it? Was he, impliedly in this email, asking - or demanding - that you lie for him to protect his image from commercial harm?"

"No, it wasn't like that at all; the email says explicitly that he had not cheated on Holly, so what dark deed of his was I supposed to be shielding?"

"You tell me. But the Larissa stories could only have hurt his reputation, Terry, so it's contradictory of Jav on the one hand to say the stories are OK and nontoxic, but on the other hand to say, in effect 'please, Terry Proudley, make sure my reputation remains good, despite the stories'."

"So what's your theory?" asked Terry, feeling a vague rising of panic within.

"My view is that he may have done something far worse than any dalliance with Larissa LaDame. So, what he was saying in the email was the Larissa thing doesn't matter, but please make sure - Terry Proudley - that you keep quiet about something far more serious."

"Well, it's a theory, I suppose," Terry conceded. "But you have nothing against me, or against Javea, so I believe it to be a futile theory!"

"It probably is, you're right," twinkled WPC Sassi. "But with men like you it pays to take nothing for granted. You seem almost innocent to me, and I hope my vibe is right. But unless you tell me all you know, well, my budding theory is likely to grow, you understand me?"

Terry had never been happier to see food arrive. The next few minutes were taken up with the staff laying hot plates on the table and bringing all the innumerable accessories which nowadays are part and parcel of every restaurant experience.

Sweet and sour prawns had always possessed a calming effect on Terry, and so it proved again tonight. The succulent, tangy flavour restored his faith in the world. Funny how his temperament could be so low and then be raised by so little.

"Aren't the police going to focus on marmalade?" he asked WPC Sassi.

The 20 year-old frowned a little. "Well, the marmalade's important, of course, but then so is checking the emails on his laptop and 'phone records and things like also talking to those he was communicating with by alternative means. We'll need to establish each and every person with a motive against him. At this stage he seems like a typical loner to me, but hopefully we'll get a lot more once we talk to Holly. But in my experience, unless Holly's the murderer - and we'll look very carefully into that possibility, believe me - I'm sure it'll turn out that he was mixed up in something that he was hiding from Holly. So, like I say, if you know something, Terry - or you know of suspects - now is the time to tell us."

"Isn't the whole thing simple?" questioned the journalist. "Judging by your strength of character, surely there'll be a pot of marmalade in Javea's house with identifiable fingerprints on it and soon your investigation will be wrapped up?"

The striking young policewoman creased up at that notion. "Like I say," she confided, "I don't know why so many people adored this guy Jav, though I admit he was OK looking. But what I've come to learn today is that many people *idolised* him! He could do no wrong whatsoever! And I stood at the entrance to Rectory Orchard cul-de-sac for hours on duty today, and his staunchest fans know that Jav is staying there! People pushed into my hands cards and gifts and love letters and whatever. Apparently Jav had earlier agreed with the Wimbledon tournament authorities that he didn't mind receiving all this stuff, and that he wanted it all simply left by us police neatly on his doorstep and he'd take it in and look at it if he wanted to. So that's what I did."

"Any marmalade there amongst the expressions of love?!"

"You bet!" remarked WPC Sassi with passion. "Two people came up to me, I could hardly tell if they were male or female, cos it was cold today and they each wore sunglasses and hoods, but I think it was one guy, one girl ... anyway, they came with a cardboard box, explained at length that they were representatives of Javea Jackson's overseas unofficial fan club, and finally shoved a box in my hands. I didn't look inside, but I'm sure little pots of marmalade were there, cos they all know their hero loves the stuff!!"

"And you left the box on Javea's doorstep?"

"Yeah, yeah, I know what you are saying. Maybe one of them was poisoned." Her olive-skinned, slim face suddenly appeared gaunt and wan. "Don't remind me, Terry, but this is why I am so determined to play an extra special part and contribution in bringing the killer to justice." She lay her hands on Terry's right hand and stared meaningfully at him. "Which is why I'm counting on you, and I'll give anything to you if you will simply help me. To be honest, given what happened today, I am nothing without you."

Chapter 11

It was a wrench for Terry to ultimately see WPC Verita Sassi depart the restaurant, by taxi, in the opposite direction to his solitary walk home. But that upset was to some extent mitigated by Verita's promise that he would no longer be required for questioning the next day, and by the fact they'd exchanged mobile 'phone numbers.

He also realised that he was personally on the brink of a professional breakthrough. His rapport with Verita would mean that he would keep close to the police enquiry, and that development would be most acceptable as far as his editor was concerned. Terry also understood that, by staying close to Sassi, he may well prove instrumental in assisting her and her colleagues in hunting down someone deemed to be a murderer. And, anyway, staying close to the silky policewoman would not be any hardship to him in any event.

The writer cheerfully contemplated the fortune cookies which had been brought to them at the end of the Cantonese feast. His had asserted: "ONLY TRAVEL WILL EASE YOUR WOES" whilst Verita's commanded her to "ACCEPT THE ATTENTIONS OF A HANDSOME STRANGER".

When he was ensconced back at home, he watched a BBC TV special on the alarming day at Wimbledon. Nearly the entire hour was taken up with an extended obituary of Javea Jackson, and at the tail end, in juxtaposition, they showed the match points won earlier in the day by Jacalyn Jeanice and lanky Angela de

Jong. There remained speculation about whether Holly would even play her first round, given her non-appearance at the practice courts.

Nevertheless, the Order of Play Committee had decreed that Tuesday's Court No 1 programme would begin with Holly pitted against an unseeded challenger from China.

Wimbledon breathed a collective sigh of relief when Holly actually took to the court that scheduled afternoon. Terry took no notes but just watched absent-mindedly as she tore through the first three games in record time against the over-awed opposition from Nanjing. His mind was fixed on potential suspects in respect of the murder of Javea Jackson and intermittently he puzzled whether a headline in the Evening Echo could be "NANJING DOING!" though he acknowledged that this pun on "nothing doing" was remarkably weak.

Whilst Holly grunted with every shot down on court, Terry took up his Mont Blanc pen and began jotting away idly. This is what he scribbled to paper:

"Central problem - anyone could have somehow got poisoned marmalade in front of Jav. The two people who handed a box to Verita may not be who they said they were. Alternatively, they could just be unwitting pawns who had no idea that the box contained poisoned marmalade.

Killer might not have cared exactly when Javea was going to die. People on the circuit, and most fans, knew he daily consumed marmalade on toast. Not exactly a sportsman's diet, but that's what he liked. In other words, even if he had eaten unadulterated marmalade for a few days, quite soon he would have eaten the poisoned marmalade and dropped dead. Many people might have known that he was overly accessible to his fans; he couldn't say no to them. So, many of them might have known that he was not fussy where the marmalade came from (although as a fitness freak it was a fair assumption that sell-by date was important to him). On the other hand, why should he be too bothered: marmalade is marmalade, right?

With that in mind, we need to look at people who may have had a motive and who also knew him well. Based on what I've learned, we have the following:

1) HOLLY FLEMING: seemed very happy when I heard her on her mobile in Eastbourne, talking to Javea. Was supposed to marry him next month. Would have been appalled by yesterday's media disclosure that he was having an affair with Larissa LaDame. Did she speak to him in between the paper coming out and Javea dying? Something for the police to check carefully. Also, did she know that Javea planned to write a book which, amongst other things, would have laid bare her technical tennis defects? How would she have reacted to that? How did she react?

2) ADELE SCHMIDT: have to include her because she was named on one of the pieces of paper given to me by Javea in Dubai. But what happened between her and him?

3) ANGELA DE JONG: Like Adele, will need to be questioned carefully, as she, too, is on the list given to me in March by Javea. Plus, did she know that Javea's book would also detail her own tennis shortcomings?

4) JACALYN JEANICE: Ditto.

5) NATALIE SLOANE: Not sure how well she knew Javea. Again, she's on the list. Rivals say she is a cold, heartless character - but is that just mindless sniping behind her back? What would she make of a book describing how to beat her?

6) DREW L TODD: A dubious agent, according to Javea, who said that the guy was, basically, amoral. Suggestion that he ruined Javea's life? How? What could he gain by upsetting Javea, who then sacked him? Are sour grapes a factor? Or more than that?

7) JON SMARTSON: The umpire tainted with criminality. Still a regular on the merry-go-round of pro tennis. Loves the limelight. Would he take action to silence Javea who had told him in Las Vegas: "One day the world's gonna know all about you!"? Clearly an unsavoury individual, given what Javea said about him plotting with a quasi gangster to capture, by coercion, a Grand Slam title for Blanca Alessandra.

8) KARAN: The Indian Bollywood star cum mafia figure. Clearly willing to kill. No doubt had heard from Smartson about Javea's "threat" to expose the would-be Alessandra scam.

9) BLANCA ALESSANDRA: Also probably told by Smartson of the threat to blow the lid off their audacious fraudulent attempt. Could she have wanted to kill Javea as a consequence?

Terry's chain of thought was broken by the spectators cheering the end of the first set. He looked up and saw that Holly had been in commanding form, winning it 6-1. The small Chinese miss looked dispirited as she trudged towards the umpire's chair.

He returned to his notes and thought that he better add Larissa LaDame. His mind went back to their rendezvous at Cafe Pergola. What was it that she had said so tellingly? Journalistic recall aided Terry. Yes, that was it: "...I can sell my story cos I was with a living legend ... only he's not living now, but that makes my story all the more valuable." Worrying words indeed. Pen in hand, he wrote:

10 LARISSA LADAME: Admits she benefits financially from Javea's death. Is that a motive for murder, by her directly or orchestrated by her shadowy cohorts?

Terry didn't have excessive time to pause on the matter. Although Holly was pushed to a tie-break in a hard-fought second set, she duly came through 6-1, 7-6 and the big question in the minds of the press guys was whether or not she would appear for a conference with them.

She did, but it was clear that the All England Club moderator would try as hard as possible to protect her from any potential intrusion. "Ladies and Gentlemen, you will appreciate that this is an extremely trying time for Miss Fleming, so please can we all act with true understanding at this moment when grief is still so raw." Besides him, the star looked red-eyed and vulnerable. "Please can we stick to questions of tennis," he directed.

There was no hope of that. A writer, not well known to Terry, yelled out: "Holly, is it true that you are going to be quizzed by the police in connection with the death? I heard from informed sources ..."

"That is enough!" exclaimed the moderator, but it was too late, because Holly replied: "I am of course willing to confirm that I will co-operate with anything asked of me by the chief inspector, but guys, there will be no more press conferences given by me throughout this tournament. You're gonna have to leave me alone. So, who wants to talk about tennis?"

The room fell dramatically silent and Ms Fleming deftly took it as a cue to make her departure. It felt as good to her as hitting a venomous smash.

Her vanquished Chinese foe was next up in the conference room. As the girl's English was limited, her comment was sparse. "She play good, but next time different, I hope. Next time I try to kill her." There was an intake of breath by all hearing her. "Sorry, I mean I try my best to beat her," said the little voice, crestfallen and grateful to disappear very quickly thereafter.

The sullen Natalie Sloane was ushered in next, because she, too, was through to the second round. She bit her fingernails nervously and avoided eye contact with the media. It was swiftly established that she would answer no questions, direct or indirect, about her dead compatriot. However, the press are canny in their approach and they made her field a question about whether she was sad today and whether she felt tennis was about to fall into decline in Britain "in light of the situation". Regrettably, she sounded harsh when she remarked in reply: "Tennis has by definition got to be about more than one individual. OK, it's a sport comprised of individuals, but the professional ranking lists go down to beyond No 1,000. So I'm not going to say tennis is permanently scarred by what happened yesterday, for the simple reason that there are too many players for a singular player that is not there to make all the difference, no matter what that person may have achieved. Personally I don't care about any other player but myself; I've got to protect my own career and do all that I can to boost it. We all take care of our individual selves."

It may have been an honest answer, but it wasn't a diplomatic one, noted Terry. He shuddered to think how the tabloid boys would twist those quotes.

Looking at Natalie had reminded him of Verita. Whilst they were both petite in height, it was the tennis player who had the less spectacular build and fuller cheeks. Moreover, there was a captivating air about Verita which Natalie simply failed to exude. Even Verita's voice seemed liked a cat purring, whilst Natalie spoke in slightly grating tones. In truth, there was a plainness about Natalie that made her somewhat unappealing. But Verita, on the other hand, was sleek, chic and fetching. Time stood still when you looked into her eyes. Terry felt that life could not be bettered when in the aura of the slim WPC.

As the day wore on, a chill crept into the air. A noisy rabble of youngsters had packed Court No 2, a playing area which Terry always related to 1979, the year when his 10 year-old self had watched televised "first Saturday" coverage of John McEnroe losing in straight sets to the unfancied Wisconsin twin, the late Tim Gullikson. It had been a sensational shock and Court No 2 thereafter revelled in nicknames such as "the jinx court" and "the graveyard of champions". Indeed, Pete Sampras' last Wimbledon singles had taken place here as well.

Today, the teenage boy fans knew nothing of '79, but had taken Adele Schmidt, the blonde from Austria, to their hearts. She and her doubles partner, a smiling Spaniard, put on an energetic display of volleying skills which triumphed in three sets.

As was the modern day custom, the sour losers strode off court immediately after a limp handshake with the umpire, whilst Adele and effervescent Cristina stayed behind to bask in the warmth of the spectators' applause. Then they spent a sizeable time signing caps, magazines, T-shirts and the oversized yellow balls that you now see at every tennis event. The victors grinned broadly for mobile 'phone pictures, but Terry, observing the scene, was haunted by the fact that Adele featured on the list of names given to him by Javea. He also recollected the incident at the Grand in Eastbourne when Holly and Adele had shown their mutual antipathy over breakfast. Why exactly was Adele on that list? And if he worked out that answer, would it point to a reason for her to kill last year's men's Wimbledon Champion?

There was an additional aspect which Terry believed to be important. Javea had amassed a fortune in his short playing career - most of it post-dated last year's title win. But who would inherit all of it? Surely the answer would yield a rich line of enquiry for the police. Simultaneously, it occurred to him that WPC Sassi deserved to be privy to all that he had gleaned from his off-the-record late night conversation with Javea back in Dubai three months earlier. He realised he had fallen for her pretty hard. He simply wanted to give to her and keep giving to her. Nothing was any pain if it led to his pleasing his new-found love. How could one person be so invigorating, he wondered? Nobody had ever enlivened him in the way she now did.

A gust of breeze alerted Terry to the lateness of the hour. There were no further matches. He reacquainted himself with his surroundings; he was sitting alone in the Court No 2 press box. The light was fading badly and the precious grass reminded him of a green sponge cake for a child's birthday. And then there was that melodious voice behind his right shoulder: "Hello once more, stranger." Terry whirled round to see WPC Verita Sassi.

"I've searched for you everywhere," she stated in a mock-displeased manner, sitting down besides him.

Terry was determined to both impress and please her. The words came tumbling out. Javea was planning a book, he told her. The death of his old coach Stan Power had persuaded the world No 1 to contemplate publishing the definitive match plans to destroy his fiancée Holly Fleming, Angela de Jong, Jacalyn Jeanice and Natalie Sloane. The deficiencies in the games of the world's top four players would be laid open to everybody.

Javea had planned to tell this quartet of women what he proposed to publish. If he had told them, added Terry, then any of them might have wanted him dead.

Verita moved closer to Terry.

Spurred on by her proximity, Terry raced on to describe the plan of umpire Smartson, film star gangster Karan and player Blanca Alessandra to undermine the entire ethics of tennis.

Verita's bewilderment encouraged Terry to talk of Drew L Todd's apparent lack of morals and the list of four names given to him by Javea. "They were all written down by Jav," recounted Terry, "Adele Schmidt, Angela de Jong, Jacalyn Jeanice and Natalie Sloane. But why, I don't really know for sure," he admitted. Fearing his companion's slight disappointment at that, Terry immediately told Verita about his assignation with Larissa LaDame, which clearly went to show that she could be bound up in any murder plan.

Then he stopped. His spiky hair seemed to be nestling against the WPC's soft locks as the distance between their heads faded away. The press box was totally secluded and not overlooked at all; Verita had checked carefully. Their eyes seemed to be swimming together.

When it came, it was a life-changing kiss for Terry which told him that he had found the woman he wanted to marry. But the clinch was a brief one. "I have a job to think of," Verita said, pulling away in haste. "Nobody must see this, I am afraid."

Chapter 12

The third day of Wimbledon gave an opportunity for the tall Dutch beauty Angela de Jong to take centre stage, along with France's latter day Brigitte Bardot look-alike, Jacalyn Jeanice.

The vibrant blonde from Paris was more of a favourite of the fans, for the simple reason that she actually seemed to enjoy interacting with her supporters. She smiled a great deal, often for no apparent reason at all, and yet it was always one of those refreshing, profoundly sincere smiles that warmed the heart of the recipient. Furthermore, Jacalyn signed a huge number of autographs. Everyone knew that if you wrote a fan letter to her, you obtained in response, without fail, an original autograph, not some computer printed attempt to fool you.

Similarly, Jacalyn also knew how to have fun, at least insofar as the watching fans were concerned. Whenever her opponents left the court for a bathroom break in a disingenuous bid to disrupt her rhythm, Jacalyn humbly sought out a willing ball boy, passed the amazed guy a racket, and proceeded to play a few points against him. The crowds unerringly loved such a willingness to have fun, and by the time the conniving opposition returned, the entire stands were rooting for Jacalyn with determined vigour, thereby willing her to victory.

At the end of her matches, Jacalyn would bring out a Louis Vuitton bag of many tennis balls, signed by her in advance, to the middle of the court. She then proceeded to hit each of the balls into different areas of the stadium, in a fervent desire to give her admirers something real with which to remember her.

Terry had asked her once about this ritual, and received an immensely logical reply: "Maybe these people have waited all day just to see me, and have taken time out from their busy schedule. Perhaps they have had to coax family or friends to come with them. So the way I see it, the least I can do is to try to put a smile on their face and give them something nice to go home with, as a thank you from me for their appreciation. Put it this way: if no-one came out to cheer me, then I would have no food on the table at the end of the day, *oui*? So I think it benefits everyone if I can show a little bit of *largesse* towards those who respect my ability; they mean a lot to me and I will never forget them."

There were some who questioned Ms Jeanice's ostensible generosity of spirit. The cynics said that her corporate sponsorships had blossomed due to this allegedly deliberate fan-friendly attitude, and that the player was simply adopting an intentional strategy in order to maximise her bank balance. When the hypothesis had been put to Jacalyn by one interviewer, she reacted moodily: "I cannot believe you are against me just because I try to give back to the community in which I operate." Even those words, declared the same cynics, appeared to be rehearsed vocabulary planted in her psyche by the domineering sports agent, Drew L Todd.

But the administrators of women's tennis counted Jacalyn as a major asset. She visited hospitals during each tour stop and sometimes impulsively donated her week's earnings to a local charity. The feel-good factor resulting from such actions was brilliant for tennis. The only problem was that perhaps the teenager had too strong a desire to want to please others - and win their affection. In addition, the other girls on the circuit were sometimes jealous of Jacalyn's character having transcended the sport. But, on the other hand, they surely had to understand that watching tennis needed to be considered a theatrical experience. Even now, lovers of the game still gossiped about the mercurial Romanian

Ilie Nastase, and how in the mid-70s he once appropriated a spectator's umbrella so that he could play on in the rain against Dick Stockton on that "old" Court No 1.

Angela de Jong, for one, was known to be tired of her French rival. Angela was a typical product of a one-dimensional childhood; she lived to win and had to win at all costs. Her looks were entirely unsullied, and with her height and willowy grace, she had obviously been called upon to light up the catwalk from time to time. Angela was happy to do this, but only if it caused minimal distraction to her tennis. Her envy of Jacalyn may well have been because, by comparison, Jacalyn was so outwardly carefree and charming, whilst Angela could seem dour and standoffish. However, in the final analysis, the average man in the street could not feel sorry for either of them; both were mega-rich and successful and remarkably attractive. What more could they want?

Adele Schmidt would have loved to boast the singles computer ranking of either Angela or Jacalyn. She still fretted that she had not fulfilled her financial goals, which is one reason why she kept battling on in tandem with her Spanish partner, Cristina. Adele had no idea what she wanted to do after playing tennis. She had spent her entire life travelling week after week from tournament to tournament, and her mood suffered whenever forced, by injury or chronic fatigue, to miss some pro event. Adele's entire existence centred around hitting a tennis ball in places all around the world, throughout the year, and yet she had an aching in her soul that told her she was entirely empty, and that all her sporting exploits hitherto were worthless, because she had never legitimised her supposed talent by winning a Grand Slam title. In consequence, her restless bid for self-acceptance continued incessantly, through all those weekly cycles.

But Terry, looking from the outsider's perspective at all the glitz and glamour, took the view that every single one of these players was extraordinarily gifted. You had to be a very special person to dedicate yourself at a young age to the uncertain hope of deferred success, and it took a strong brain to maintain focus through all the tough contests, setbacks and outside difficulties which followed. Having said that, what a privilege to give yourself so fully to one cause, thought Terry.

He was back at the All England Club to cover the developments of day three of the Championships. The temperature had suddenly shot up exponentially and there was conjecture that the Centre Court thermometer would reach 100 degrees. That, Terry pondered, was tennis at its best. Two players desperate for glory; their games evenly matched. The rank and file hushed and expectant, anxious to see the duel before them, and then the final denouement. An unrelenting sun beating down to make the athletes' mission more burdensome only heightened the suspense...

Terry felt that his own affairs were reaching boiling point, too. WPC Sassi had had to leave him hurriedly after their rushed kiss the previous evening, but he had no desire to sidetrack her from her police duties, and he didn't want to hamper the police's unmasking of whom they thought was Javea's killer.

Before the day's major tests on the show courts commenced, Terry - as was his wont - meandered around the tournament's peripheral activity, glimpsing the encounters on the outer courts. He wore low-slung faded blue jeans and a fashionable white shirt. It was, at times like this, an especially relaxing life - even more so when he considered that he might have ended up as a lawyer in a dull corporate existence, worrying frightfully about "statutory time bars" and whether his client's interests would be irrevocably harmed if, for instance, the opposition employed nefarious delaying tactics to frustrate the beginning of an arbitration process. It didn't bear thinking about.

He experienced a secret injection of calm as he reflected on his good fortune, and he began watching play on Court No 3 from a vantage point to the right of, and behind, the umpire's chair. The protagonists were so near to him that he could easily see the perspiration on their skin when they changed ends in front of him. Terry began to immerse himself psychologically in the battle before his eyes, until he became aware of someone standing unreasonably close to his left.

Feeling his body tighten, Terry slowly looked round to find himself studying the taut jaw of the agent, Drew L Todd. Even on this day of burning heat, the New Yorker was dressed in a grey pinstripe suit, along with sinister black shirt and matching black tie. The guy looked as if he had lost his way en route to Wall Street. Drew's hands were deep in his pockets and he was chewing gum vociferously. Terry found the agent's green eyes piercing, cold and unnatural.

The journalist gazed back at the court, not really willing to engage in any conversation with this suited spectator. But, again, his very being tightened as Drew tapped him on the shoulder. "Hey man, we should talk, I reckon. I saw you the other night with that lady from the cops; she's a real honey."

Terry was deeply uncomfortable and could already gauge that other people close at hand were listening in to the agent's patter. Resenting the tanned presence, whilst simultaneously determined to find a more sequestered place to converse, Terry raised his eyes to motion Drew in the direction of Court No 6.

They walked together, with Terry snapping slightly: "Well, of course I talk to the police; you must have known from Monday evening's press conference that it was they who wanted to talk to me."

"That's just it," drawled Drew, as they sidestepped fans that were in their path. "Why would a somewhat nondescript scribe such as yourself be worthy of that kind of attention?"

Terry chose not to rise to the bait. "Oh, you know," he replied, glancing at Drew. "Us nondescript folk can surprise people from time to time."

"So - what do you know?" quizzed Drew L Todd, suddenly snatching control of Terry's left arm. "And how much have you heard from Javea?"

The reporter, disturbed, pulled away from the American and

73

moved smartly towards the perimeter fence by Court No 6, a spot where they could communicate in relative privacy. "I'm sorry," said the agent, his voice now low. "I just think that the police must want to talk to you for a reason, and as you're a Brit, you must have travelled from time to time with Javea. Accordingly, I guess that you must have had a lot of idle chitter chatter over many years with the dead man."

They were now looking at Court No 6, with their backs to the wall bordering Somerset Road. Terry realised that Drew L Todd would not be shaken off lightly. The guy's reputed pushiness and persistence were again coming to the fore. "I hardly knew Javea," asserted Terry. "I thought it was you, Drew, that had the connection, albeit only business-wise, with him."

Terry flashed a quick look in Drew's direction, but the latter was looking straight ahead, his eyes seemingly only for the tennis on Court No 6. There was a silence between them, punctuated only by a welcoming slight breeze, which penetrated the arid, humid atmosphere.

It was Drew who eventually interrupted the quiet impasse. "Look, there's a few things you oughta know. Many people could suffer fallout in light of Javea's demise and someone like you, clearly with a degree of involvement in the police process, can see to it that the innocent do not suffer."

"And you're one of the innocent ones, right?"

"Right; I have to protect my mercantile persona. Terry, you would not comprehend that I am nothing without my clean reputation. Clients like Jacalyn will also be affected detrimentally if I am put under the official microscope, so…"

"So what do you want?" barked Terry, taken aback at his own impatience.

"All I am saying is that whatever you might have heard about me from Javea; well, it's not true, and furthermore I had nothing - *nothing* - to do with his death. I'm requesting you to convey that to your English police force friends."

"And if I don't?"

The face of Drew L Todd scowled belligerently. "That would be most unfortunate," came the response.

"Are you telling me Javea was wrong about you, Mr Todd?" asked Terry calmly. "Was he wrong when he made a cryptic comment to me that you were wholly amoral?"

Drew seemed to find the words themselves intrinsically painful; his features contorted. "What has he told you?" he questioned dramatically.

"I know," responded Terry. "About the book."

"You do?"

"Sure; and I would say that Javea's death came just in the nick of time for you, Mr Todd, wouldn't you?"

"Don't threaten me," shot back the agent. "No-one liked Jackson! He was a troublemaker who deserved…"

"What? Death?"

Drew stared menacingly at Terry; the latter was a man gaining in confidence and composure by the minute. "You have no comprehension, Proudley. What about Adele Schmidt? What about Jacalyn Jeanice?"

"Oh, you're about to tell me that your own client is mixed up in Javea's death, are you? That's very confidential of you."

"I don't care about you, or what you think," fumed the New Yorker in reply to the sarcasm. "Fact: I overheard Adele saying that she would like to see Javea dead!"

"When?"

"At the Essex House hotel in Manhattan! When Javea was playing mixed doubles with her at the US Open last year! They were odds on to win it; the field was diluted and weak. No other big names at all. Why he decided to play the event was a mystery; Adele's on her way right down, and he didn't need the money. Some say he was just using the doubles for practice. But then big ace Javea decided that he was injured one day, so he pulled out of the mixed. Yet the next day he was fine enough, and greedy enough, to continue playing for himself in the singles! So Adele was majorly bummed as Javea had effectively robbed her of what she always desired - a Grand Slam win! It took her ages to try to get over it; she feared that true success would forever elude her. Word has it that she was devastated for weeks."

"And then what happened?"

"She decided to get even."

Terry paused. "And Jacalyn?"

Drew sighed. "You need to do your homework about the circuit, Terry. You should research your stories and take some pride in your performance. Don't you know anything? Admittedly I only know the mere outline, and I'm sworn to secrecy regarding the little I do know. After all, as you say, Jacalyn is a client. But I believe I am correct in saying that she has had some dark obsession, which is possibly ongoing, about Javea Jackson. God knows what she may have put him through. But my guess is that it borders on the pathological. And that is all I know," added the agent, straightening his tie and running a hand through his short hair. "But whatever Jackson might have told you, you can now tell your police pal that Drew L Todd should not be, and must not be, suspected; if they want people to harass, then tell them to try Jacalyn (without mentioning my name) and that mad woman, Adele Schmidt."

Suddenly, Drew was just a retreating figure fading into the throning crowd. He had given Terry information that needed to be relayed back to Verita; some pieces of the jigsaw were now fitting together. But Terry's luck was in short supply. Throughout the entire day he saw nothing of WPC Sassi. His only joy, therefore, was creating a vivid report from Wimbledon on the continued progress of Angela de Jong and Jacalyn Jeanice. The Evening Echo's own news reporters were now camped out at the tournament and Terry left them to pen a combined piece about the official investigation. Apparently Javea's laptop had yielded no clues; he had only just purchased it, and the singular email sent from it was to Terry. No emails had been received.

Chapter 13

Thursday promised to be another boiling day at the Wimbledon Championships. Even at 9am Terry could feel the rising heat in his small studio flat in Heathview Court, a quiet purpose-built block located off the busy Wimbledon Parkside road. At most, it was a peaceful 15 minutes on foot to the All England Club and usually he was like an excited child as he made his daily way to the hallowed centre of the tennis world.

But the death of Javea was always there at the back of his mind. It was difficult to relax at the tournament when you had no idea whether or not you were conversing with a killer, or with someone close to the killer. Given that Javea had opened up to him "off the record", Terry ardently believed he carried some sort of moral burden to bring the murderer to justice. It seemed so unlikely that any fan, however deranged, would want Javea dead, because his name had never been associated with such unwanted groupie attention. The compelling truth was that the obvious suspects were all too apparent, and they existed in the core of the tennis milieu.

The reporter reflected on the previous day's altercation with Drew L Todd, an agent who had something he was desperate to hide. But what? Perhaps Drew had been involved in some truly shady deal that had struck Javea as completely unforgivable. Whatever it was, Drew patently had an unpleasant streak. Terry thought back to the repellent way in which his arm had been snatched; it was a warning. And it hadn't escaped Terry's attention that the American had been determined to cast a rumour of culpability in respect of whomever he could suggest. It was plain that the names of Adele Schmidt and Jacalyn Jeanice had been forcibly impressed upon Terry in the hope that, in turn, the police officers such as WPC Sassi would cast their net of suspicion away from Drew.

Terry knew that time was on his side today, now that the news boys from the Evening Echo were responsible for reporting all material developments on the criminal enquiry. Terry was consequently charged with the relatively easy task of injecting some humour and happiness back into the tennis with light, frothy tales from the tournament. That made everything manageable and elementary; all he had to do was string together player post-match quotes to try to make the whole event as entertaining and "human" as possible. No-one wanted to read about backhands and forehands, especially at times like this.

So, feeling professionally untroubled, the journalist decided to take a morning walk. His flat in Heathview Court was directly opposite the Wimbledon Common, with its 1,100 acres of pleasing, unfenced greenery.

He had always enjoyed it there. In the heart of the placid common, you could forget that you were in busy London; you could look around for 360 degrees and see nothing but natural heathland. He loved the fact that one could lose oneself completely amongst the woods and dense shrubbery, and look at numerous ponds, the golf course and a picturesque windmill. A nearby pub had an unaffected, old-fashioned ambience, which filled him with glee.

But today the glee in his temperament was roused for another reason. There, standing on Parkside by the horse-riding path leading into Wimbledon Common, was none other than the teenage maestro herself, Jacalyn Jeanice. Furthermore, the youngster was in full riding outfit. She smiled and waved as he walked towards her.

Jacalyn wiped her palm on her jodhpurs, then warmly shook Terry's hand. "Hi, how are you?" she asked sunnily.

"I'm fine," answered Terry. "But what are you doing here?"

It transpired that Jacalyn had a secret passion for horse riding. "Y'know, I noticed one time that there were stables in Wimbledon Village so I thought I'd give it a try. Even experienced riders can work out in this beautiful park," she enthused.

"But you look like you're waiting for someone."

"We agreed that my driver would pick me up here at nine, but whaddya know? He's not shown."

"Why horse riding?" asked Terry, ignoring the issue of the errant chauffeur and instead sensing an offbeat story that might look good in the Echo.

"Funnily enough, it's all to do with tennis," replied Jacalyn. "You'll know of course that in the 1950s there was a very great, very young female tennis star, an American called Maureen Connolly."

"I do," concurred Terry. "She won the Wimbledon singles three years straight, '52 to '54. She was the best ever."

"Right. And then she never played here again. It's so sad, so poignant. Anyway, she had a love of horses and when I was young, reading about tennis, I wanted to copy everything about her and everything she did. If Maureen loved horses, then I'd love horses."

"But you know what happened to her, don't you?"

"Of course, yes. I think that after she won her first Wimbledon the people of San Diego, her home town, gifted her a horse, whom she called Colonel Merryboy. One day a truck driver recklessly crashed into Maureen on the horse, and that was that. Her tennis career was over. The leg was shattered. And later, after having two beautiful children, she was struck by cancer and died in her 30s."

"It always amazed me," sniffed Terry, his eyes a little watery in reaction to the pathos, "that, according to Maureen in her autobiography, Colonel Merryboy was not in fact injured by the truck and stood loyally by her, unscratched."

"*Incroyable*," murmured Jacalyn. "Both death and autobiographies have preoccupied me a lot in the last few days. Come on," she continued, endeavouring to be more cheery, "let's go back into the common and walk down towards the Wimbledon Village entrance, if you know the way."

Terry signalled his agreement and felt somewhat light-headed in the company of the star beside him, but he had to admit to himself that the French player was lively and engaging. She began to convey to him how absorbing and consuming she found life on the tennis circuit, and added that charity work and the horse riding gave her some distance from the all-demanding business on court.

"So why think of death?" Terry remarked.

"The fact Javea's gone is hard to take in," said Jacalyn. "You have to really wonder about who might have had it in for him."

"You have ideas?" asked Terry nonchalantly.

"*Bien sûr*. Some people just saw him as a piece of meat, a meal ticket, nothing more. There has to be a day of reckoning for them."

The pair walked on. "So you had no real connection with him?"

"Do we have to talk about that? He meant a lot to me but I did not mean a lot to him. It happens. But what can I do? So many people want me," she continued bitterly, "so many. And yet the one who actually meant something to me - the one I wanted - he was outside my pathetic grasp."

"How does that make you feel?" (It was a rather lame offering, but it was all Terry could muster to fill the auditory void which followed Jacalyn's words. He was sympathetic, yet curious.)

"I've kept up with the latest reports. If you're asking does it mean I wanted to poison marmalade and kill him, I think you need to know that I did not. But now I have to play on knowing that some will suspect me. I'll never feel free until the criminal is caught. And I also know I'll never be free of Javea's memory. I think only once in a lifetime can I love someone in such a way, with such intensity."

"Was it hard for you to know that he was about to marry Holly?" questioned the writer. "Was that the most difficult thing to bear?"

"Naturally, I felt awfully strong distress, and bitter, violent jealousy. I'm not going to deny it. But in the end I love Javea so I had to let him go, even in the knowledge that I was the best person for him. I couldn't have harmed him. I couldn't bear to see him, it was like a deep pain every time I saw them together, but I swear I never did anything to endanger or cause problems for Javea. He made life worth living for me, even though my passion was forever unrequited, for reasons I'll never understand."

It transpired that Jacalyn's ardour for Javea stemmed from when she met him for the first time in England. She was a happy-go-lucky adolescent who had never before travelled overseas. She came over from France, by ferry, for a series of junior tournaments. Her English was basic and she arrived unaided and unescorted, hungry for excitement.

Jacalyn quickly spotted handsome, personable Javea, who evidently had near hero status amongst both his male and female tennis peers. Her initial enthusiasm for him turned into an infatuation, which steadily progressed to a preoccupation. Depressingly for Jacalyn, the reality was that over the months and years that followed, Javea merely smiled courteously and exchanged pleasantries with her, but the encouragement she yearned for never became forthcoming.

"It is true I am on fire for him, even now," confessed Jacalyn. "I have constantly tried and tried to get him out of my mind, but thinking about him made me happier than actually being with someone else. I suppose Javea was that massively magnetic to me. My belief is that you can only feel that heightened craze for one person in your entire lifetime, and for me that person was Javea, even though he literally disregarded me in the end, although he remained impeccably polite most of the time."

Terry and the celebrity walked on through the alluring countryside close to the hub of London. "I tried too hard to get him," revealed Jacalyn. "You know, I used to 'phone or text him when he was playing the men's events in other parts of the world. I sent him expensive white gold gifts, many of which I personalised by engraving his initials and so on. I showered him with jewellery, clothes, aftershave, everything I could think of to give him rapture and delight."

"You can't buy love," stated Terry simply.

"Oh, but you can try," asserted Jacalyn. "There was something about him; his compassionate eyes, kissable skin, the lilting voice that made me feel he understood me on some deeper level. I wanted him to find me sensual and slinky, but you know what? I reckon that deep down he pitied me and considered me desperate. That is the bit which hurts the most."

"In a way, it must seem less complicated for you, now he's gone." Terry knew that it was a provocative statement, which risked Jacalyn's fury. But the girl was talking as if she was in a daze, and it was time to break the spell.

"Mr Proudley, I should be infuriated by your accusation. But truthfully, I'm not. Because the actuality is that you are quite correct. It comes down to the old adage - if I can't have him, no-one should have him!"

Her penetrating blue eyes flashed with a dogmatic force; Terry automatically knew that it would be prudent to change the subject, at least to some extent.

"You said earlier that you'd been thinking recently about autobiographies; why?"

"Ha! That's an easy one. You can blame Javea for that as well. I get this call from him a few weeks ago when I'm playing in … I don't know, Berlin, I think. It excites me to hear from him. And then he starts speaking in an official way, telling me that he's writing a book and part of it will be spilling the beans about what coach Stan Power believed was the unknown way to beat me, Natalie, Angela and Holly!"

"How did you feel?"

"Humiliated, *oui*. I had all this fascination, this adoration for the guy and his focus was on unveiling my trade secrets to all his readers! He defended himself, saying something about my appreciating it would spice up the game. But the only spice that would have interested me was leaving the circuit for six months, going to Mauritius or wherever, and spending every day with him. It was a kick in the butt; but I presume that Javea never actually began his book and so now I'm spared from all the up and coming players learning my flaws."

"You frighten me," said Terry. "You seem so frustrated with your life. It's as if you are…"

"Vacant? Well, I am. I wanted something that I could never get. But, like I already told you, none of that makes me a killer. Javea was forthright and controversial. His way of doing things wasn't the way most other people did things. So what he did was antagonise *beaucoup de gens* a lot of the time."

"Such as?"

"Look at my agent, for one. Drew couldn't even look at Javea after the two of them parted ways. Talk about a beautiful trading relationship gone sour! I swear that Drew actually twitched bodily when he saw Javea recently. There was definite bad blood there."

"Any reason why?"

"No-one knows the whole story, but after the split, I figure that Javea had some hold over Drew. Drew is not a prepossessing man; you must know that. He does what's best for him and cloaks it behind a mask of bonhomie. But he's the most insincere human I know."

"So why are you his client?"

"I made a mistake. I'm gullible, I'm prone to it. Yes, I have lots of faults - just like idolising Javea. I fell commercially for Drew's line of chat that suggested I was the most important person to him in the world. I regret it now, but the fixed term of my contract with him ends at the close of this year, and I won't renew. He can't stop me, anyway."

"He knows this at present?"

"No, of course not. But I think he's already living in fear of his network of riches crashing down. Tennis players are fickle; they soon move away from someone out of favour. My deduction is that if Javea was planning to write in his book as to why he really hated Drew, then Drew would have definitely wanted to silence Javea. So I hope the police study Drew as their number one suspect. OK, OK, I know I'm currently contracted to him, but please understand me, I have a healthy distrust of him."

"Well," Terry replied, "I think it is true that Javea's book would have explained his animosity towards Todd. What I'd be interested to know, from you, is your speculation as to what it could possibly be about."

"Off the record?" pronounced Jacalyn, suddenly a shade wary.

"Obviously. All of this is off the record."

"I am certain that Drew L Todd is a racist," uttered Jacalyn. "He has no black players on his books. I imagine that this would have appalled Javea, who took such a significant issue very seriously indeed. My guess is that Drew's racism prompted Javea to cancel the contractual relationship between them. No doubt Drew made some explicit remark to Javea on the subject of race, which transformed Javea's suspicion into cold certainty."

"So you think Javea may have been planning to quote racist comments from Drew in the book?"

"*Absolument*; that's what I'm saying. But now I'm getting tongue-tied over all this. I know, I've got a good idea - let's jog the rest of the way!"

It was much-needed exercise for Terry, and besides, he didn't want to see Jacalyn disappear just yet. But it's always difficult to keep up with a professional sportsperson, and within minutes Jacalyn Jeanice had vanished from his sight.

Later in the day, Terry watched as Thursday's contests saw victories once more for both home favourite Natalie Sloane and world No 1, Holly Fleming. But the drama for the Evening Echo's newshounds revolved around the fact that the police were telling them that a female living in the Channel Islands was about to be interviewed in connection with the murder of Javea Jackson.

The identity of the lady was, however, not being revealed. Terry didn't tell them that the net was obviously closing in on Blanca Alessandra, and that he wanted to be there when it did.

Evidently WPC Verita Sassi had corresponding aspirations for Terry. A couple of hours later, he received a text message requiring him to telephone her. When he did so, the writer was immediately disconcerted by the weariness in Verita's voice.

"I have literally been working all hours," she complained. "I can't tell you too much about the enquiry - some things have to be hush-hush - but the general consensus is that someone mixed up with the Bombay underworld is perhaps more likely to kill than an admittedly cut-throat bunch of professional tennis stars. So, all thanks to you, I've been dispatched to Jersey tomorrow to interview this Greta Garbo character. What's her name again?" Terry heard rustling of paper.

"Blanca Alessandra," he reminded her.

"Right. British Airways leaving Gatwick 11.55am tomorrow." Verita paused. "Why don't you come along? Meet me at the North Terminal."

When in love, people often opt for what is overly ambitious. Terry was no different. Mentally he banked on the fact that freelancers at the All England Club would be more than happy to impart enough dope to enable him to write his next day feature; that, coupled with post-match quotes, should suffice. His editor need never know he had been absent from the first Friday of Wimbledon. Furthermore, if he could persuade the Echo's photographers to strive, just this once, for some creativity and originality, no-one would lose. But Terry was conscious that his chicanery may nevertheless come to light if either Jacalyn Jeanice or Angela de Jong sensationally lost their respective third round bouts.

"I'll be there," he assured Verita, whilst at the same time thinking of Jersey's sandy beaches and the fact that it was basically a British place, which gained character having been influenced by the Italian, Spanish, Dutch, Portuguese and French. It then unexpectedly hit him that his developing devotion for Verita bore disquieting similarities to that Jacalyn had had in relation to the dead Javea. After all, Terry was now skipping work and sensing only too well his rising possessiveness towards the coquettish cop.

Chapter 14

Flight BA8037 to Jersey with the uniformed WPC Sassi seemed like a hallucination for Terry. Every second of their one-hour journey was tinted magical, as if imbued with pervasive enchantment. The most mundane actions filled Terry's heart with jubilation. Whilst the overworked air hostess behind him in economy class struggled with the drinks trolley, he, in contrast, couldn't help but feel that everything was ideal with the universe.

Then he remembered that Wimbledon was mourning the death of its male Champion and that his liaison with Verita had been caused purely by the ongoing murder enquiry. He stole a look at his consort and observed that she was tired and strained. Beyond her, he could see through the small window that the plane was passing through thick, dense clouds.

"What's so wrong?'" he asked.

Verita stared back at him testily. "I am a professional and a perfectionist, and I've got to find the killer," she countered. "And so far, that's not proving possible."

"Any luck finding that couple, the overseas unofficial fan club representatives who brought the box for Javea?"

"You mean, the ones who handed the box directly into my exact hands," she shot back. "Not yet. I feel morally responsible for his death. If only I had checked the contents, none of this may have happened."

"You're exhausted and overwrought," replied Terry softly. "Even if you'd studied the box, you wouldn't have detected that the marmalade was poisonous, would you?"

His words partially reassured the young policewoman. "You're right: I am anxious and jumpy. I desperately want to prove myself at work."

"The whole thing now seems so complicated," admitted Terry. "Drew Todd's been stressing me out, saying that the police must not suspect him because the real suspects should be Jacalyn Jeanice or Adele Schmidt. Jacalyn, according to him, because she had a crazy unrequited love for Javea, and Adele because he overheard her saying she wanted to see Javea dead. Then, less than 24 hours later, Jacalyn informs me that Drew is probably a rabid racist and had violently offended Javea on the subject."

"So Jacalyn thinks Drew is the culprit?"

"Exactly. But they say hell hath no fury like a woman scorned. I still think that Holly must be the most likely candidate for murder because she would have hated finding out about Javea and Larissa."

"But," responded Verita slowly, "the email you received from Jav said that he hadn't been unfaithful to Holly."

"Maybe he was lying," offered Terry.

"Well, you needn't worry," confided Verita. "Holly is in fact set to be arrested as soon as her participation in the tournament is over. It was on the chief inspector's advice that she's not giving any press conferences since that original one. And as a mark of consideration to the tournament, we're currently holding back on interrogating her. The tennis establishment is desperate for the women to put on a great show in the absence of the men, and in the last few days there has been huge behind the scenes political wrangling because their argument is that the women's world No 1 is required to be playing at her best ability in order to show off the women to the best extent possible. So we're not troubling her and we're holding back, but if she tries to fly out of London when her involvement in Wimbledon has finished, we'll be there to collar her."

"I think Holly is the key to this," reaffirmed Terry.

Amused, Verita gave him a smile. "So what's all this 'hell hath no fury' rubbish? Surely that could equally apply to Adele Schmidt, especially if you're telling me that Drew heard her say she wanted to see Jackson taken out."

"True," relented Terry. "The reality is that none of us really know what anyone else is going to do when they believe they're under real pressure. You see, Drew comes across as not a nice character, and if Javea was going to kill his image, who's to say that Drew wouldn't have killed Javea first?"

"Absolutely, I agree," said Verita, "but the best police bet is that an Indian underworld figure is probably the assassin of Javea. You have to admit that the argument has a certain level of convincing coherence."

Before the correspondent could reply to her, they both felt the plane experience oscillating turbulence, and then the public announcement: "Ladies and gentlemen, the captain has switched on the 'fasten seatbelts' sign, so please return to your seats until he decides that we are past this rather bumpy phase of our travel. We regret that unfortunately the washrooms are closed during this period of time until further notice."

Verita and Terry discontinued their discussion. Instead, his mind wandered to the island of Jersey, just 14 miles off France's north-west coast, and Queen Victoria's phrase: "What a pretty, rich country this is." The police had been shrewd in their detective work, which had ferreted out Blanca's whereabouts. Terry recollected that Javea had told him that Blanca had exhorted the young competitor Javea to play a tennis event at least once in Jersey. It now looked as if Blanca had escaped to this island haven to regroup and reinvent herself after her unfortunate brush with a Bombay gangster and a twisted umpire.

"We're off to St Brelade," interjected Verita playfully, as if reading his brainwork.

"St Brelade?" answered Terry blankly.

"St Brelade's Bay, to be exact," continued Verita. "Our former tennis star apparently has some superlative living quarters at a hotel called L'Horizon which is situated in the bay. I'm told it's breathtaking. White sands, dramatic seas. Sounds too good to be true, doesn't it?"

"Though I note from our tickets that we're not staying the night," said a rueful Terry.

"Life's a bitch, isn't it!" Verita parried in a jocular tone. Terry had no rejoinder to that.

Chapter 15

The descent into Jersey was long and ponderous, with the jet constantly buffeted by topsy-turvy storm conditions. They seemed to be struggling forever in the choppy air, and the eventual landing was a bouncy, irregular affair - although not bone-breaking.

As they dismounted, the passengers were met by forceful winds and driving rain. Verita frowned in distaste, but Terry smiled at her. He had always found dark clouds, haze and mist to have an indefinable romantic quality. He also hoped that play at Wimbledon may be badly affected by the inclement conditions; that would nullify any potential for him to miss any surprises.

Verita and Terry took a taxi from the tiny Jersey airport and were soon on their scenic way to the L'Horizon Hotel. Within minutes, given that the island measures only nine miles long by five miles wide, they passed the Norman church at St Brelade, which dated back to the 11th century, and then came a tantalising glimpse of the rough sea. Next, on the right and set back from the road behind some trees, stood the white building where Blanca Alessandra reluctantly awaited them.

Terry, ruminating on the fact that the Nazis occupied Jersey for five years, was caught unawares when approached in the hotel's reception by a large lady wearing a shocking purple velour tracksuit. Her face was prematurely wrinkled and her hair bleached blonde. But most of all it was the fleshy physique that unnerved Terry.

"Hello, do I know you?" he asked cautiously.

"It's me, I presume, you both want to talk to," came the brisk reply.

'Blanca?" he queried, uncertain.

"Please come with me," said the lady in a bland tone, looking at both Terry and Verita.

So this was the formerly gorgeous Blanca Alessandra, concluded Terry, a little shaken. The dynamic looks of years gone by had faded markedly, and it was astounding to see her so overweight and her sun-damaged skin akin to parchment.

The trio advanced up the luxurious staircase to the second floor. Half way along the dark corridor, Blanca opened the entrance to her ritzy suite. The windows spanned from floor to ceiling and they faced directly onto the blustery beach and the sea, which was overwhelming in its frenzied turmoil.

Blanca motioned her visitors to a functional sofa, and sat herself in a homely armchair. She stared momentarily out to sea, then considered Terry and Verita. "So, you're here because Javea Jackson's perished, yes?"

Verita responded: "That's right, Blanca. The deceased was murdered five days ago, on Monday. Mr Jackson had previously told Terry here that there was an unfortunate effort to try to derail tennis from its tracks."

"Ha! I got wind of all this from the umpire, Smartson. Quite unbelievably, Javea chose to threaten him during a match itself! Something like: 'You won't get away with this!' Something crazy like that. And Smartson, quite without my desire to know about it, contacted me to warn that Javea might be stupid enough to tell the world about a dirty deceit that never was."

"It was more than a deceit," argued Verita. "As I understand it, tennis officials were bribed and your rivals endangered. Even now they're too scared to speak. Didn't you care about all that 'play up and play the game' stuff?"

"Are you trying to provoke me?"

"The point is," said Terry, "that you admit you knew from Smartson that Javea might be about to publish something. So you were fixed with that important knowledge before Javea expired."

"You're saying I had something to hide."

"Well, didn't you?" retorted Terry.

Blanca thought for a second or two. "I have already lost everything," she ultimately answered. "I knew that Karan and Smartson were both demented. I was simply too timid. Of course, I should have tried to get away from Karan earlier, but have either of you been on the receiving end of love from a crook? The worry is permanent - night and day - that if you try to break away, a person like that will come after you to kill you. Why exactly Smartson was also so underhand is something that I cannot fully fathom. But I repeat: I've already lost my life and dignity. I live here because I cannot face anyone. I walked away from tennis, which I loved, because Karan would have hounded me at every tournament and the other pros would never have forgiven me. So I had to go on the run. The official story was that I had family funeral issues and debilitating injuries. But I didn't want to be a gangster's moll all my days, and to disappear was the only hope for my safety and sanity. Yes, I hate Javea for bringing up all this past history - I despise him for it! And I don't care that he's dead, because he should have left me in peace. But having said all that, you are way off the mark if you think I had anything to do with the stupid man's slaying."

"Then who did?" demanded WPC Sassi. "Because from where I'm sitting you are horribly mixed up in all this. You completely admit to having underworld links, and the underworld likes to butcher people. So I am not going to light up and let you plead your innocence; it makes me sick."

"Look, I know nothing," pleaded Blanca.

"That's not good enough!" stormed the policewoman. "You spent years of your life with a likely murderer and you're telling me you have absolutely no idea of who might have killed Javea?"

"It wasn't me," stressed the fat woman, leaning forward in her chair. "But you guys have got to talk to Smartson. I don't know what it is about him, but I reckon he's far more inherently evil than Karan. You'd be startled, but there undoubtedly is something totally wicked and cruel about him. Perhaps Smartson had hoped that Karan would get bored with me and then donate me to him; perhaps that's why this nerdy umpire was so favourable to Karan's plan to buy me a Grand Slam. At least with Karan there were moments when he was fun loving and courteous to me. But Smartson: he just leered at me. And look at it this way; Karan is probably far away from London, but Smartson is right there in the thick of it at Wimbledon. I've seen his repulsive face on TV this week."

"When did you last speak to Smartson?" Terry quizzed her.

"No comment," parried Blanca. "That's it, I've already had enough of this. You're not getting any more from me. Ever heard the phrase 'blood from a stone'?"

"So you've talked to him very recently," asserted WPC Sassi. "And when was your last contact with Karan?"

The statement received no response. A quiet stillness filled the room. Resolute Blanca was stony faced, but conversely both sensitive and thin-skinned at the same time. She repeatedly fidgeted with the heavy silver bangles on her wrists. At last, after what seemed a lengthy silence, Terry and Verita jointly decided to leave. Blanca wasn't going to volunteer anything additional on this visit. They muttered their departing words and in a flash had left behind the weary "yesteryear female talent", as Javea had described her to Terry.

"She seems innocent to me," grumbled Terry, as their car took him and the policewoman away from the L'Horizon. "She's evasive, but only out of dread, I think."

"I don't agree," replied Verita. "These people can protest their innocence and yet of course they would, if they've committed murder. And she's probably still regularly in touch with Smartson. I can envisage that she, Karan and Smartson may have all conspired together to kill Jav, if only out of sheer malice. It could be that the three of them all contributed to the scheme. I don't want you taking everything that is said to you at face value. After all, these are merely initial interviews."

Terry admired the firm rebuke in her voice, but was pained by the fact that Verita, on duty, was a total professional who showed him no sign of her seductive skills. However, they forgot about crime during a leisurely Indian lunch of king prawn dupiaza at a cafe called Elly's in La Pulente, which had a superb outlook to sea where surfers normally relished the waves, and after that they were driven through scenic, remote, narrow hilly roads to the white Corbiere lighthouse. The tableau was comforting to Terry: they emerged from the car and were at once struck by a gale, rain lashed down ... and all of this amidst striking rocks and crashing waves. He took a mental snapshot and banked it for a future day when he might be suffering sadness. At the same time, it reassured him at that moment to remember when Martina Navratilova had once arrived at Wimbledon in a Rolls Royce whose registration plate carried the affirming words: "Love Conquers All". Seeing Verita laughing, with the lighthouse as the backdrop, it seemed totally appropriate.

Chapter 16

Friday at Wimbledon had been dominated by black skies and ongoing rain. You had to feel significant sympathy for those who had planned in advance to take time off work, rise very early and join the queues outside the All England Club at about 6am. Such individuals were life's enhancers, happy to spend four or five hours chatting with their friends whilst awaiting entrance to the greatest tennis show on earth.

Time was passed for them by eating, drinking, sharing gossip, checking the daily order of play (to see who was due on the outside courts) and collecting a seemingly endless amount of free promotional gifts from a ceaseless amount of hawkers who had things to give away. Blazered club officials were on hand to deter any would-be queue jumpers.

Despite the downpours, the static troops calmly stood in line; they were hopeful of seeing tennis. Excitement grew at around 10am when the gates were opened, and one by one the fans swarmed into the Wimbledon grounds, full of expectation and ambition for the day ahead.

But that foretaste steadily diminished with the passing of the next few hours. At first there was pleasure derived from simple admittance to the venue. After that, there were strawberries and cream to indulge in, and programmes to acquire. The club's souvenir shops enjoyed the bleak weather, with so many mortals determined to part with their money in exchange for an item bearing the Wimbledon trademark. School children were elated by the array of pens, pencils, erasers and key rings on display. Occasionally, delight was then had in spotting a tennis celebrity dashing through the showers in a bid to both stay dry and avoid autograph seekers. However, by 5pm, most people were leaving the tournament, heading to either Southfields underground or to Wimbledon station.

Play was officially abandoned for the day at 6pm, meaning that Terry hadn't missed a ball swatted in anger. The Evening Echo had an easy job; they revived the Daily Express 1980 headline "SWIMBLEDON!" and filled their pages with photos of scantily clad female fans, together with a nice shot of Jacalyn Jeanice and Angela de Jong putting aside their differences and grinning under a multi-coloured umbrella.

For Terry, the evening was one of mixed fortunes. At Gatwick, Verita had told him, quite rightly, that she had to go back to work and report on Blanca Alessandra. She wanted time to collect her thoughts and make notes before her meeting with the chief inspector. As a result, she left by separate taxi and Terry took another taxi back to his flat by Wimbledon Common. Yet on the way home his poise was maintained by the last thing Verita had said before leaving him at the airport. She had kissed him tenderly on the cheek, and purred: "You really are an angel, Terry. Thanks for not being mad at me; I respect you even more for that."

He was also heartened to receive a late night 'phone call from Verita.

"Look," she said, "a few days back you were asking me about marmalade. I guess it is the key to the whole case. Do you want to know - confidentially, I mean - the latest on that?"

"That would be really something," Terry responded. "We keep meeting suspects - Drew, Jacalyn and now Blanca - but the whole riddle is troubling because any of them could be responsible for arranging the poisoning of Javea. Obviously there's no point asking them where they were when Javea died because the murder weapon was the marmalade alone, not someone who physically struck him. I've always felt that they all had opportunity to get a poisoned product to him, so motivation is what's significant, not the…"

"Marmalade?" replied Verita, laughing heartily. "So the exact opposite to what you said earlier, you mean!"

They collapsed into simultaneous hysterics. "Now do I get into the police force?" joked Terry at last. "I've proven my credentials!"

"You are one contradictory bloke," chided WPC Sassi in coltish fashion. "Well, I'll put the 'phone down as you're obviously not really interested in what I've just heard about the poison."

"No, no - I am," said Terry strongly. He continued in a playful, innocent way: "I guess if you're investigating a killing - even informally - it pays to know as much as possible about how the murder was committed, right?"

"Right - something like that!" chuckled Verita in response to his sarcastic self-effacement. "So, here goes; I hope this isn't too complicated for simple little you."

"Ha, ha," Terry replied to the teasing young woman.

"Apparently, in Javea's flat they found a pot of marmalade with fingerprints, just like you said they would."

"So, I am a detective," cut in Terry.

"Or a killer," said satiric Verita.

"No, but there had to be fingerprints, didn't there, I mean that's always how killers are caught, right?" came the defensive retort.

"Whatever. But the scenario is tougher because *TWO* marmalade pots in the Rectory Orchard property were found to be poisoned."

"Doesn't that just mean that whoever did Javea in was making doubly sure the job got done?"

"It's certainly one possibility, Terry. But the conflicting fact is that the two pots were of different makes and expiry dates. It appears to our people that the two pots were not necessarily connected. One of the pots has no fingerprints and appears to have been in the box from the fans. The other pot has fingerprints."

"Whose are they?" whispered Terry.

"Should I tell you over the 'phone?" asked Verita, suddenly speaking in an anxious manner.

"I don't think this place is bugged," smiled Terry. "Come on, it looks like this matter is almost solved. Whose fingerprints are they?"

Verita gave the name to Terry, whose automatic reaction was unprintable. "That person now has to be the top suspect," he added.

"Not definitely," said Verita. "At the moment it looks like there is a different type of rat poison in each of the two pots. And it seems as if two differing sets of people wanted Javea dead. It's also proving hard to determine which was the pre-poisoned marmalade that was, as you say, the murder weapon."

"If only we knew more about these fans," replied Terry, "we could probably eliminate them from the enquiry. They're probably harmless obsessives who…"

"Aren't obsessional people more likely to cause harm along the way?"

"Well, I see what you mean, but they're probably just harmless fans…"

"Obsessives, fanatics: same thing, same problem," warned Verita.

"OK," accepted Terry, "but the point I am trying to make is that the 'fans' are probably innocent and someone has duped them to carry a pot of poisoned marmalade. Hopefully, if you find them, they'll be able to focus on whom it was that gave them the poisoned one."

"Possibly," said Verita, "but it's unlikely. They're an unofficial fan club. That means people probably just posted them stuff and the fan club founders simply said they would be going to Wimbledon and would try to deliver the things to Javea. All very amateurish. I would think it's a remote chance that, even if we find the fan club leaders, they're gonna know anything about how they happened to receive poisoned marmalade."

The truth was demoralising to Terry. He shared the police-woman's zeal to nail the murderer, who had - now it seemed obvious - a fair chance of evading penal sanction due to this intricate web of ambiguity which threatened to stall the investigation. Having said that, the name given by Verita was surely that of the individual who put the lights out permanently on Javea Jackson. Terry knew he would sleep badly, and he blamed Jon Smartson for that.

Chapter 17

Possibly it wasn't only the unpleasant tennis umpire that prevented Terry from dozing off. His repose was additionally thwarted by Verita Sassi, the alluring, comely girl who was taking over all his thoughts. He realised that his longing for her was like a terrifying but bizarrely enjoyable physical pain. To rely on her was heaven, but to think of that reliance dropping away was hell. Terry worried whether or not Verita was falling for him like he had already fallen for her. He wanted her to belong to him; only then could he always be at peace.

Deep down, Terry believed that he lacked the necessary social skills, happiness and *joie de vivre* which he presumed Verita demanded in a mate. His real fear was that he was gauche and depressing, and he was wary that if his true self became known, then Verita would run a mile. His deliberations were exhausting.

He still felt miserable the next day when he awoke. He wondered whether this would be his permanent life state; forever fearing disaster, perpetually pensive that whatever the moment offered, it was not enough to banish his gloom.

Perhaps the writer should have guessed instead what it was like to be umpire Jon Smartson. The latter man was thickset and had a visible paunch. Divorced and childless, his sanity, such as it was, hung by a thread, dependent on an everlasting itinerary created by a continuous diet of international tennis tournaments. Smartson knew his years were sinking away and that he was deteriorating all the time. Whatever looks he had had were now lessening quickly; he had an inkling that he was devoid of real charm. But he maintained a lifeline by remaining involved with pro tennis stars, and he envied their youth, looks and hope. Smartson lived vicariously via these rich, striking, juvenile celebrities.

Terry was in no mood for games when he chanced upon lonely Smartson sitting outside the officials' complex close to Court No 2. He decided to confront the underhand official.

Smartson looked up with dirty, globular eyes as Terry approached. The umpire was drinking a black coffee and had a cigarette in his right hand. His whole demeanour came across as shifty and wayward.

"Terry Proudley, how are you?" said Jon with false enthusiasm. "Well, it's really Super Saturday today, isn't it. All that rain yesterday and now the crowds are in for a treat! All the top four female lovelies in action on the very same day!"

Terry sat down opposite him and looked into Smartson's corrupt eyes. "This must be a trying time for you, Jon," opened the writer.

Smartson tried to effect stupefaction. "Well, I'm going to be in that high chair for more hours than usual today, I suppose."

"Oh, I don't mean the umpiring," continued Terry. "But I agree it'll be hard for you to concentrate given all that you're involved with."

The sinister eyes blinked back at the journalist. "What exactly are you talking about?" asked Smartson. "Here, are you secretly taping me, because if you are, I'll…"

"Pipe down," ordered Terry. "No, I'm not taping you, but I've got your number all right. And I want to know all that you know about Javea Jackson's death."

Smartson's podgy face scrutinised his interrogator. Then there was a bitter, short laugh. "I have no idea what you expect me to know," came the eventual reply.

"Let's just say that Javea spoke to me a few months back. He mentioned your name. Told me some very interesting material

- which I believe is relevant to the circumstances surrounding this week's murder."

Smartson twitched uneasily in his chair, and inhaled deeply on his cigarette. He looked over at the club's main concourse and then exhaled a plume of smoke. "And what exactly would Jackson have told you?"

"About Las Vegas, for instance."

"Las Vegas," echoed Smartson, stubbing out his fag. "Well, not much happened there, buddy boy. Javea kept foot-faulting, I kept noticing it, he lost his stack so I had no option but to warn him for racket abuse. Hardly a reason for me to kill the chap, I'd say!"

"What did Javea actually say? Tell me that," instructed Terry firmly.

"I dunno, to be exact. These prima donnas will shout anything to anyone in the heat of the battle. Even curse their grandmothers, they would. But it's all got precious little to do with me."

"Unless, of course, they exclaim to you directly and explicitly in front of a whole stadium: 'One day the world's gonna know all about you!' Pretty strong stuff, I'm sure you'd agree, Jon."

The umpire looked uneasy and once more visibly twisted himself in his chair. He lit another cigarette. "Oh, did he say that? Probably he did. Just goes to show he deserved a penalty point; I'd forgotten why I'd docked him one."

"All right," replied Terry evenly, "let's cut all this crap, shall we. You know full well that what Javea meant was that he would one day blow the whistle on your vile attempted scam with Blanca Alessandra and that Indian Bollywood star cum gangster, Karan."

Jon Smartson's face turned ashen and pale. For a second it seemed he was going to be sick. "How do you know about that?" he urgently questioned Terry.

"Because Javea told me about it. And if he had published it, your days of touring tennis events with all expenses paid while each week you call a few balls in and out would be well and truly over."

"What else do you know?"

"Why don't you tell me about Angela de Jong?"

"What about her? I know nothing about her other than what everyone else knows. I have had no involvement with her whatsoever. She has a boyfriend."

"No involvement?" queried Terry meaningfully.

"No involvement," fumed Smartson. "And if you're daring to insinuate otherwise, you'll be hearing from my lawyers this afternoon. This is slander and it's a disgrace. How dare you? Are you threatening me? Are you trying to destroy me? The Alessandra thing is in the past; I couldn't help being got at by a bloody mafia guy! And as for Angela, you've got a nerve to even…"

"Dare to tell the truth?" asked Terry confidently. "You were rumbled, mate. By Javea. In Melbourne. When Angela left your hotel room. Don't tell me she never told you?"

Smartson looked panicked, as if he was fighting for air and for his survival. Terry pressed home his advantage. "Alessandra told me yesterday that you notified her of what Javea planned to do; ie disclose the failed fraud of the three of you. Clearly it was a great worry to you. Equally, having an affair with a competitor would totally destroy whatever you have left, particularly if her boyfriend found out. So there are two compelling reasons why Javea's death would have saved you, agreed?"

"Blanca had as much to lose as me. More even, as she was a public figure," raged Smartson in defiance. "I don't earn much money, either. That means if my fling with Angela became public, she'd lose a fortune, so her motivation is also far, far stronger than mine. Look, I'm a nobody, a nothing, so spare me. It's the affluent and the powerful who rule the cosmos, so go and hassle them, not small bit characters like me."

The interview was over. Smartson stormed off. The journalist remained quietly seated alone at the otherwise vacant table, even some minutes after the tirade was over. He glanced from time to time at the boisterous tennis fans and couldn't help thinking that, like Smartson, he, too, was perhaps a zero as well. It was enough to further ache his tormented heart.

Chapter 18

Holly Fleming, America's darling, opened the spectacle on Centre Court. She was small for a world No 1, but her frame was angular and, perhaps today, verging on being a little skeletal. Her usually shiny skin lacked radiance and even her normally precise curls were looking dishevelled. Terry remembered all the times in the past when Holly had flashed a broad grin and revealed her pearly white teeth, but he could make out that the girl was currently uptight and under pressure.

He also knew that Holly often received lucrative offers to undertake modelling assignments, but at 21 she had thus far refused them all and remained steadfastly committed to striving for sporting eminence.

It was no shock to Terry, who understood the game better than nearly all the press corps, when Holly struggled against her third round opponent from Japan. In the first set, the heroine made repeated unforced errors and virtually gifted points on a plate to her rival. 6-1 in 19 minutes was a horrid start for Miss Fleming, who grimaced with discomfiture.

On occasions thereafter Holly seemed to be locked into some distressing hypnotic mode. She raised her eyes to the skies after missed shots, and Terry speculated that the world No 1 was having difficulty thinking of any reason why it was worth playing the game. At 1-6, 2-5, Holly was about to be annihilated. But having hidden her head in a towel at the changeover, the pretty warrior emerged as a different person. She started fighting with distinction and honour. Every point captured was greeted with a clenched Holly fist.

The Japanese disputant raised her own levels of performance in retaliation, but it was apparent that Holly had mentally resolved to rule with an iron hand. Winners streamed from the American's racket as she started to suppress the uprising. Holly seized the second set in a tie-breaker and suddenly it was her rival who had the air of one who was tyrannised and downtrodden.

Holly reeled off the last six games to take the third and final set, 6-0. The stands were still buzzing animatedly when she strode off court, ignoring the outstretched pleas for autographs from the front row seaters.

Next up on Centre Court was Natalie Sloane, the British favourite. Without delay, the stout lass was overwhelmed by the chanting of her name and by the patriots' faces painted with the Union Jack. She determinedly kept her eyes staring at the turf beneath her feet as she walked to the umpire's chair and set down her rackets, almost oblivious to the carnival atmosphere and the unruly Mexican wave.

Every time Natalie hit a shot over the net in the warm-up, the mob bawled their encouragement. When she removed her tracksuit top before the first point proper, there were admiring wolf whistles and cries of "Natalie, marry me." Her opponent seemed to shrink and disappear, rejecting the jingoistic setting. Terry could discern the defeatist body language a mile off. And Natalie, on the other hand, duly obliged her loyal subjects, raising her arms aloft about an hour later in recognition of her straight sets' obliteration of the petulant Scandinavian on the opposite side of the net.

Over on Court No 1, leggy Angela de Jong's features, and play, had both been flawless. She booked her place in the last 16 in a flurry of balletic strokes that emphasised her supple skill and lithe form.

Afterwards, Jacalyn Jeanice waved to the fans when she took to Court No 1. She winked at a ball boy and gave him a heart-fluttering smile before serving. She blew a kiss to a lines-judge when the elderly gentleman called a 50:50 decision in her favour. And, as ever, having subjugated her opposition, she hit her autographed tennis balls all around the stadium, and even gave more signatures when leaving the playing area.

It had definitely already been an extremely successful Super Saturday by the time a somewhat listless Terry filed his report on the day's four main duels. But he lacked happiness and didn't fancy sitting later amongst the Centre Court faithful to observe Adele Schmidt's ladies' doubles clash. He had always found it irksome to try to concentrate on watching tennis when he was stressed. Instead, sitting in the media centre, Proudley passively experienced pang after pang of desolation bludgeoning him.

It was, therefore, very fortunate that he received a call on his mobile from WPC Verita Sassi. His heart thumped wildly and his throat turned dry. He took the call and could feel pinpricks of sweat materialising on his palms.

"Tonight," started her enthralling voice. "Why don't we get together? I'll be off duty in five minutes. Think about it, then ring me back."

The line cut. The conversation - or should that be monologue? - had lasted about four seconds. But instantaneously Terry felt lifted, invigorated and rejuvenated. The desperate agony in his stomach miraculously abated and his brain sparked back into an inspired mood. Verita actually likes me, he thought. I am worthwhile; people want me!

Someone else wanted Terry. The mobile sprang back into its own form of life. The caller id showed that it was Terry's editor demanding a word (or two) with him.

The harsh snap in the editor's chat was missing on this occasion - replaced by an almost immature, quirky quality. "Karan," the over-anxious editor breathed, "Karan has rung the Evening Echo - our switchboard. He wants to meet you. Tomorrow. In India. Can you make it? He'll be at the Taj Mahal, shooting a film there all day or something. He says any funny business and you'll be killed. But you have to go, have to go. Find a way to get there and get back by Monday! These are orders, Proudley - make sure you follow them! So hurry up, get on with it! You understand?"

Terry fought hard in a bid to swiftly assimilate the overload of information and his own astonishment.

"Yes, yes, of course I understand, I'll get on to it right now. Thanks: this, er, this could be good for the paper and for me."

The editor answered in an uncertain monosyllable - "Right" - and terminated their conversation. In the calm that followed, the oppressed journalist felt that he was constantly battling those who had the ability to manoeuvre him like a puppet on a string. In this instance, however, the realisation didn't make him feel tragic; this time he adjudged that something good could actually come from being victimised.

Terry appreciated he was going to immediately ask Sassi to join him on this whistle stop trip to India, and his childish joy was further exacerbated by the comprehension that he would be face to face with a Bollywood film star when he reached there! Such a set of circumstances struck him as really living life. Soon he would be gaping at the world's premier landmark to love, accompanied by his one *raison d'être*. He began dreaming of nights by the Yamuna river, with the Taj Mahal behind him bathed in moonlight, and Verita cheek to cheek in a dance with him… On top of that, he fantasised about hot days, a burning sun, brilliant blue skies and Sassi hugging him; together they would contemplate the awesome white marbled structure… The journalist subjectively decided that nothing could beat having his photo taken with Verita at the Taj Mahal; it would be his crowning achievement, simply too good to be true. What was life's purpose, anyway, unless the things happening to you were too good to be true? Terry was sure he knew the answer to that question.

Chapter 19

There followed a whirlwind 24 hours for Terry and Verita. And it was the latter's impressive energy and drive that made the sojourn to India possible.

As soon as the conscientious officer heard that the temperamental Bollywood star was willing to talk, she swung into action, always mindful of Terry's need to be back in London by first thing Monday morning.

Verita received Terry's call, explaining everything, at about 6pm on that Saturday night. Terry had no idea how the trip could be organised, but Verita - strong-willed and steadfast - was adamant that this opportunity to build lines of communication with Karan must not be lost.

For Terry, it was a dream come true to be so accepted by Verita and to have a mission in life - to win the WPC's heart and to determine the person understood to be the killer of Javea Jackson.

It was beneficial to both the journalist and the policewoman that Karan was calling for an encounter on Sunday. It meant that Terry could relax in the knowledge that there was no play at Wimbledon and Verita was free of any desk-bound office duty that day. In any event, it was simplicity itself for her to obtain official Scotland Yard approval for the trip. The top brass were, in truth, beginning to clutch at straws. The enquiry appeared to be going nowhere, with every "discovery" turning into a sombre blind alley. Officers thought - just as Terry had - that it would be a breakthrough once it was known who would inherit Javea's colossal fortune. But it turned out that Javea was bequeathing his entire wealth to a number of charities working in West Africa, including the World Health Organisation. The verdict was bleak: no-one close to Javea would benefit financially from his death.

The dramatic rush to the Taj Mahal began with an 8.30pm evening flight on Gulf Air to Muscat, Oman in the Middle East. Luckily, they had no option but to travel light, given that they would only be in India a few hours. As a result it was easier for Verita to arrange for them both to be fast-tracked through the security checks at Heathrow's Terminal Three.

"We'll be there in no time," she said to Terry reassuringly, once they were buckled into their business class seats. "Arrival at Muscat at 8am local time; that's 5am UK time. I've pulled some pretty cool strings to have us flown from there by some small plane - perhaps a 16 seater - direct to Agra in North India. The commercial flights just didn't work out. A lunch time flight on Gulf to Bombay, and then to Delhi, then another separate flight to Agra would have lost us too much time to be back in London by Monday morning. That's why I've arranged for our special plane to wait for us in Agra, and then as soon as we are ready, we'll be whisked back to Muscat. Hopefully we'll be there in time to grab the midnight Muscat time Gulf flight back to London. In that case, we'll touch down back here at Heathrow at about 6.50am Monday morning UK time. Am I a genius or am I a genius?"

No-one needed to tell Terry that the stunning Verita was a genius. Her ability to make him deliriously happy meant she was mesmerising to him. Equally, the svelte policewoman fed his ego with her desire to learn from him.

"Tell me," she asked, shortly after their take-off out of London. "We've got Holly, Jacalyn, Angela and Natalie. Jav planned to disclose all their tennis flaws in an autobiography. Are you telling me that these clever girls and their support teams have no real understanding how to beat each other?"

"It sounds unlikely, I know," volunteered Terry. "But you'd be surprised that I watch tons of matches and it's clear to me that the players are often clueless about how to exploit their opponents' weaknesses. I mean, they simply don't seem to see the weaknesses. It's sort of funny, because from where I'm sitting, the way to win is obvious."

"But if it's obvious to you, why aren't you out there coaching?"

"Good question. I guess because I've not achieved anything in the world of tennis. And these pros only want to listen to past Grand Slam victors or else coaches who can hit a fierce backhand and rally with them on court. I can't do either of those things, sadly. And I agree with those who say Stan Power was awesome; he was a truly great coach. But in my mind his lifetime principle of client confidentiality meant that he failed to help his charges exploit the faults in their opponents. You see, at the very top of the game, they are all basically as good as each other at hitting the ball, but if they really understood what it would take to hurt each other, then the person who understood that would win time and time again, in my opinion."

"Give me some examples," said Verita, turning to look into Terry's eyes.

"Examples? Um, OK. Well, I've watched matches where it's blindingly apparent to me that one girl can only slice her backhand; she can't attack with her backhand at all. So, all you've got to do to beat her is hammer the backhand side and get to the net. But guess what? The other girl stubbornly decides to keep feeding her forehands, thereby completely failing to capitalise on the defensive sliced backhand. It was madness to me, watching it. And then I've seen a girl with an obvious inability to run wide to her forehand side. This means that you should aim to place balls wide of her on the sideline. But again: guess what? The opposition chose to play the whole game hitting down the middle of the court. This meant that the player who made an error every time she had to run wide to her forehand never had to worry too much; because 90 per cent of the time the balls were played into her comfort zone, right down the middle of the court. I can give you another example. A player who…"

"No, no - that's OK," interrupted Verita. "I think what you are saying is that Stan Power had the instinctive knowledge of how to comprehensively beat each of his students. He chose, rightly or wrongly, to keep that wisdom locked inside his head. That is - until near his own death when he communicated it all to Javea. What you are saying is that the Power expertise would have been decisive, and could have blown apart the career of at least one of those four girls."

"Exactly. The reality is that the players, by and large, do not take enough care to play their rivals' weaknesses. One of those four girls may have been particularly threatened by the thought that her problem areas on court were about to be published. But it's late and I'm getting very tired. Do you want to try to sleep a little?"

"Not just yet," replied the slender policewoman. "I want to understand as much as possible. It's clear to me now that the whole 'exposing of the tennis weakness' thing represents a true reason why someone might kill. But right now we have to think of Karan. What is his mindset in all of this?"

"Yeah, it's good to talk this out," responded Terry, trying to hide his fatigue. "You know that I spoke to Javea off the record in Dubai in March. He had stupidly threatened Jon Smartson on court with the words: 'One day the world's gonna know all about you!' As Javea explained it to me, his very real concern was that both Blanca Alessandra and Karan would hear from Smartson about the possibility of being exposed. Although the scam ultimately came to nothing, this guy Karan was hardly going to thank Javea if a book came out portraying Karan as a lovesick puppy who was determined to impress Blanca through violence and coercion."

"So there we have it," agreed WPC Sassi. "You're very cogent. Karan had every reason to want Javea dead."

Soon after that, Verita fell asleep, with her hand softly holding one of Terry's. It should have acted as a balm to the writer, but instead he felt stressed within. In the murky aircraft cabin, he pieced together the combined learning of himself and Verita. He hadn't wanted to admit it directly to the WPC, but he would of course do so before they spoke with Angela. Yes, he couldn't forget that back in Dubai Javea had written down Angela's name as being the girl who was having a clandestine relationship behind her boyfriend's back with none other than umpire Smartson. And then Drew L Todd had made it apparent to him that Jacalyn Jeanice was the one obsessed with Javea, and Adele Schmidt hated the men's No 1 because he allegedly cheated her out of a Grand Slam title. Terry felt somewhat guilty that he hadn't disclosed to Verita that, by process of elimination, Todd had also unwittingly shown that it was Natalie Sloane - the player who didn't look like a player - that was, if Javea could be believed, a drug taker.

In contrast, Terry realised that Verita had been very upfront with him, especially in that 'phone call when she had told him that one of the poisoned pots of marmalade carried the fingerprints of Holly Fleming. He had to admit that things looked very black indeed for Holly. No wonder she was to be arrested when her Wimbledon finished. She had suffered humiliation because of the Larissa LaDame story and that could easily have translated into her desire to kill Javea with poisoned marmalade. Terry wanted to believe that Holly was innocent, but how could she be? Terry took the view that Holly, broken-hearted by the Larissa article, must have realised that a marriage to Javea was doomed. Robbed of what she hoped for, she must have flown into a rage and resolved to knock off her fiancé with rat poison.

But, Terry thought, the situation was complicated by the existence of a second pot of poisoned marmalade with no fingerprints. It seemed that, independent of Holly, someone else also desired the liquidation of Javea Jackson. The lack of fingerprints pointed to a more professional would-be murderer, and - in consequence - Karan had to be seriously in the frame. The possibility was also there that Karan may have forced Holly to take poisoned marmalade to Javea; in such a scenario, the question would be whether or not Holly had any notion that she was a collaborator.

Yet still loose ends remained. Terry made a mental note to ask Verita again whether there had been any joy in trying to find the two fans who had passed her the box for Javea. After all, Verita was certain the box contained pots of marmalade, and the official view was that one such pot, *sans* fingerprints, had been laced with rat poison. This was the so-called "second pot". It occurred to Terry that Karan could have been instrumental in getting both the first and second pots in front of Javea. The more Terry thought about it, the more he felt sure that Verita was right - Karan was behind all of this.

When they landed in Muscat, Terry was tense, knowing that Oman was bordered by Saudi Arabia, Iran and Yemen. But all he could see when he emerged from the Gulf Air 'plane was a large strip of runway, white airport buildings and rocky mountains ringing the ancient city. He had read in a travel magazine that when in Muscat you are supposed to stay at the sumptuous Al Bustan Hotel, a coastal palace of cathedral-like proportions. But he reluctantly accepted that there was no time for romance; the Omani police authorities hurried them in the blistering 50 degree heat to what seemed like a tiny jet and in a matter of minutes he and Verita were again airborne, bound for Agra, which had been the capital of India back in the 16th and 17th centuries.

As they headed to the city 200 kilometres south of Delhi, Verita spoke about Karan. She had clearly done her homework since the murder took place. She explained to Terry that Karan was treated like a god in India, having starred in a great number of popular Hindi blockbusters. The moviegoers would see any film in which he appeared. They saw him as being able to play convincingly both comic and more serious roles.

Verita continued: "India's got more than a billion people. Karan is the most bankable dude in the Hindi film world. So in fact he's the most popular film star on the planet. On the plus side for him, there is mass adulation. Thirty-five thousand fan letters a day, I'm told (or surely they mean per week?), anyhow, most are from females desperate to marry him. On the negative side, a lot of Bollywood films are financed by the underworld and Karan cannot escape them. He probably pays them protection money, but the thing is the gangsters love Bollywood stars and the stars are in the thrall of the gangsters. There's a blurred line between them. The point is that Karan can call on muscle if he wants it; he's also seriously rich. You know rich people - they get bored. He can choose any girl he wants in his own country, but guess what? Apparently Karan has a thing for more Western, European style beauty. So Blanca fell naturally into his sights."

"And perhaps Holly did, too," offered Terry. "I've been wondering whether our Bollywood hero may have used Holly as a conduit to get poison to Javea. Maybe she knew that's what he intended to do, or maybe she didn't. Either way I now think you're probably right - Karan's used to getting what he wants and would have hated Javea for being on the brink of ridiculing him in print."

"Seems feasible to me. But remember that Karan is used to bad publicity. The Indian film magazines are full of his antics every month; he beats up girlfriends, boasts of his underworld connections, and ends up in drunken brawls all over the world."

"Sounds like a pretty wholesome guy," laughed Terry. "Meeting him should certainly be an experience."

"Don't expect this to be funny," shot back Verita. "It sounds like you've got visions of Indian films involving overweight blokes in naff jumpers, yodelling away and unable to dance. But that's all changed - this man Karan is as cool as you could hope to meet. A delicious torso, pecs to die for. Muscles in all the right places. Never seen in public unless he's in serious designer gear. Drives the flashiest cars money can buy. Facially he's all about angular cheekbones and searching brown eyes, so…"

"I get the picture," replied Terry tersely. "Changing the subject slightly, if he has all these links to the gangsters, how is he able to operate without getting caught?"

"That's a question you should have asked me back in UK," said Verita. "Let's just say that money can buy lots of things, plus Karan usually does his stuff via go-betweens. He's not stupid; he knows the art of self-protection. But with Blanca it all became personal. Seems to me that Karan basically became one pining mongrel. Aren't men pathetic when they're ruled by a woman?"

"Ho, ho," said Terry, with mock bitterness.

"Seriously," continued WPC Sassi, "I'm really sorry that we are not yet getting proper time together, Terry. I feel the same way about you as you do about me. It's just that, like I say, I'm a perfectionist and I have this pointless need to control my environment. I love you, but till we get Jav's killer, I have to remain professional and not get involved. I feel really bad about this; you've gotta blame my nature. When we've solved this crime together, let's really be together. We'll fly far away from UK so that I can lavish all my time on you. How about it?"

Terry was quick to agree with her strategy. But, once in Agra, as they made their way through forgettable streets by black Mercedes to the Taj Mahal, he couldn't help but feel a little jealous about Verita's analysis of Karan's good looks. It was obvious that the film star would be everything that Terry wasn't: carefree, stylish, ultra-slim, effortlessly hip and an awesome dancer into the bargain. It didn't bode well.

It was hellish for Terry that when he finally saw the majestic domed Taj Mahal from an archway just inside the red sandstone gateway, he was unable to simultaneously take Verita's hand and lead her closer to the bench where all the tourists - including Princess Diana - have themselves photographed for posterity. If Terry had had his way, he would have slipped a huge diamond engagement ring on Verita's tiny finger just as a camera clicked. It would have made a memorable picture, especially with the 74 metres-high building, and the four minarets, reflected in the clear blue pond behind the bench.

But there was business to do. Instead of sharing the hypnotising symmetrical spectacle with Verita, their eyes were instead drawn to the male star of the silver screen, Karan, gyrating away on the grass in front of the Taj's central structure, flanked by a group of female dancers clad in camouflage-coloured tight shorts and halter tops. The area was roped off from tons of bystanders, and Karan was giving passionate looks to each of his dancers as they all moved in perfect time to the addictive loud backing music of rap infused with disco melodies. The film crew were calling for take after take in the gruelling sun, and Karan's job was the hardest because he had to conjure up the right emotive expressions whilst lip-synching to the Hindi lyrics.

A thin Indian boy in his late teens sidled up to Terry and Verita during one of the innumerable breaks in shooting. He introduced himself with pride as "Sachin, Mr Karan's spot boy." Sachin noticed the quizzical looks caused by his words, and added: "Spot boy. I am like Mr Karan's personal assistant at any outdoor shooting. I get his food, his drinks, his cigarettes, his clothes. I have to do what I am told."

"What's he singing about?" asked Terry.

"This is all part of a new flick," clarified Sachin. "The Hindi title of the film translates in English to something like: '*I love you ... to death*.' Indian people are no longer interested in dances round trees and family dramas. This film is very good. Shalini is Karan's co-star. She's a heroine here. You don't know Shalini? She's a ten, man, a ten. Anyway, in this song Karan is very upset. He plays a college boy in love with Shalini's character. But Shalini's mother hates him and splits the two of them up. The mother tells false stories to the girl to persuade her to love another boy. I don't know how the film will end, but I think Karan's character will end up killing the other boy because he's so madly in love with the Shalini girl. Cool, na?"

Inwardly, Terry thought that the movie could well be an instance of art imitating real life. It was a comfort for him when finally the filming came to a halt. WPC Sassi pushed through the hordes and pulled the writer along with her. There was a trace of recognition in Karan's deep brown eyes as he saw the couple approach him, with Sachin attempting to walk beside them.

Verita marvelled at Karan's well-sculpted physique, rippling beneath his skin-tight beige Versace top. Terry detested the hero on sight. Karan just burst into laughter. "Hey, yaar!" he exclaimed to Terry. "I've seen that little passport photo of you in the Evening Echo when I'm in London! But who's this amazing chick with you?"

"I'm his wife," replied Verita. "I'm Verita. Pleased to meet you."

She stuck out her hand. Taken aback, Karan laughed once again and then, looking a little abashed, shook hands with the policewoman.

"Why are you saying 'yaar'?" Terry asked Karan. The reporter smiled at Verita, then added: "That phrase went out of fashion in the late 80s. It's what the city slickers in London's financial district used to say: 'OK, ya'."

"You're joking!" said Karan theatrically. "Here in India, 'yaar' means 'friend'. And you're my friend, Terry, you and your beautiful wife here."

Having dismissed his spot boy, Karan insisted that they all go back to the presidential suite at the nearby Taj Amarvilas hotel. Terry made sure that the three of them were taken there in the black Mercedes that was theirs for the day, driven by a white-uniformed chauffeur who was respectful and deferential at all times.

"This place is more Hollywood than Bollywood!" wise-cracked Karan as they entered the palatial apartment at the top of the Amarvilas hotel. "Musharraf stayed here when they had an India-Pakistan political summit. Can you imagine, the leader of Pakistan sitting here looking at the Taj whilst drinking his drink!

Let me show you the bathroom; it's too special, man. The shower is huge; it's one big glass conservatory and even that has great Taj views as well! Maybe it was when Musharraf was taking a shower that he fell in love with our Taj!"

Karan, so full of manic energy, fixed himself what appeared to be a quadruple whisky and sat back on a leather armchair. Terry and Verita - making do with less comfortable, more formal chairs - each declined the offer of drinks, although both were dehydrated and impatient.

Karan suddenly seemed to understand his guests' disquietude. "Terry," he bellowed after a large slurp of whisky. "You want to know why you're here, yeah? You and your lovely wife. Because I know all about Javea Jackson's planned book and I've also known for a long time that he told you what he was going to do. You met him in Dubai, correct? Yeah, well I've been aware of that for months."

"How?" asked a puzzled Terry.

Karan laughed like a crazy maniac. "I don't think I have to threaten you overtly, man. You know what I am capable of organising if you dared print any of this. But I still love tennis; the whole circuit, the razzmatazz, the jet-set lifestyle. It's just like the films! Me, I'm in Mauritius one day, Bombay the next, then Goa, after that Switzerland, London. Tennis is showbiz, same as Bollywood! So I keep in touch with developments. Let's just say that some friends of mine are able to get an inside track on the tennis stars via certain electronic gadgetry. I know every piece of gossip on the tennis tour. Between you and me, if you monitor a few hotel rooms, it is a real eye-opener!"

"So why bring me here?" appealed Terry.

"Because it's fun for me to see the guy who thinks he might have found out what happened to Javea Jackson. And because it amuses me that I may in fact be suspected by you. But print any of this and I'll have you killed. You're here just so I can make you understand. Do you really think I care if some dude prints a book claiming I tried to bribe tennis umpires and threaten some of the players? Everyone would be too scared to give any evidence against me, and Smartson and Blanca I could have taken out if it became necessary. So I'm not your killer, and if you knew enough about the stars of the women's game, you'd realise that they are the ones who had the real axe to grind. Me, I'm used to having a bad image and reading wild stories in the papers that I have underworld connections and so on. This is Bollywood! I can't control who contacts me, and I'm not going to discuss my friends with you either, you understand?"

Karan was becoming increasingly hostile as he continued drinking his whisky. He kept refreshing his glass from the bottle by his feet. Yet Terry still quizzed him: "What is your fixation with tennis really all about?"

"It's a release for me, that's all," acknowledged Karan, more quietly. "And it's glamorous. Plus, I've always liked to control people. I like to know what's going on behind the public facade. So the private lives of public figures captivates me, and tennis will forever be special to me, because of Blanca."

"Could Smartson or Blanca be killers?" enquired the newshound.

"Not Smartson, no way. That loser is a weasel. For me he was just a way to get to the game's establishment and make it known that I wanted Blanca to win a Grand Slam. But Blanca is different. I thought we would be together for life. I told her never to betray me. But she got away from me and if anyone should be murdered, it's her for disappearing when she was supposed to stay with me. So she's cunning, and she cares a lot more about what people think of her compared with me. Would she want Jackson eliminated if he was about to bring to light the fact she knew what Smartson and I were getting up to? I think she would. At the moment she can live in denial, wherever she is, and try to forget me, our mutual plan, and Smartson's part in things. Other than a number of people in the tennis world, no-one knows that she was mixed up in a fraud that was about to happen. But Jackson's autobiography would have shamed her in front of society as a whole, and I have no doubt that Blanca would have wanted him dead instead of facing such dishonour. But me, it's water off a duck's back. I can take negative press - in fact I reckon my price in crores goes up every time the media has it in for me."

"So you think Blanca is a more likely murderer than Jon Smartson?" questioned Terry.

"One hundred per cent. Smartson is zero, although he's having a fling with Angela de Jong, you know? He hasn't learned his lesson at all after being linked with my scam! But it's Angela that's using him, for sure. She's deliberately trying to make sure she has friends on court when the going gets tough in a tight match. Added to that, I can tell that she gets adrenaline from doing what she's not supposed to do. Her boyfriend is another who'd kill if anyone ever tells him that Angela is cheating on him. That girl is playing one dangerous game!"

"And she knew that Javea's book would explain how to beat her," added Terry.

"That's true!" smirked Karan. "I know about that, too! So she had a double motive to kill Jackson. But even the Brit girl, Natalie Sloane, was furious when she heard that the guy's book would detail all her problems on court. And she's got a second motive as well. The girl's taking heavy-duty drugs and so far she's getting away with it! But if her addiction was put into the open by Jackson, her endorsements and career would bite the dust straight away! Which only goes to show that there are three ladies - not Karan - who wanted the end of Jackson."

"You don't have suspicions about anyone else?" asked Terry.

"Nobody. I don't know about any others. After Blanca, I lost interest in the game until Angela came along, so that's why I've made it my business to know all about her. I heard about Natalie from, er, let's just say a mutual pal. And that's everything, guys. I've told you all I wanted to say. Time's up."

Verita and Terry could register that they were being dismissed. Karan's vehement denial was plausible, but how could he really be believed? Terry decided to raise one more point. "Karan," he said, "what's your relationship like with Holly Fleming?"

"She bores me. I don't know her. She was besotted with Jackson, but I could never see what he saw in her. Now get out of here, and don't print a word of any of this. Not unless you want to end up like Jackson."

It wasn't a particularly harmonious note on which to leave, but Terry felt that it could have been much worse. At least the death threats had only been meted out verbally. And he had seen the Taj Mahal with the girl he was going to marry. It was also good that Verita had said nothing at Karan's; her silence was subtle and meant that Karan had, for all intents and purposes, ignored her.

They reached Muscat in time for the midnight (local time) flight back to London. Verita slept. How cool Shah Jahan had been, thought Terry, to build the Taj as a symbol to his cherished wife who died. However, the world's greatest love affair was tinged with sadness; the workers who built the Taj apparently had fingers amputated so they could never build something similar again, and even Shah Jahan was locked up in Agra Fort for the last few years of his life, only being able to see the Taj landmark through barred windows. Terry concluded that it would have been really something if Shah Jahan had managed to construct a mirror image black marble Taj Mahal as his own mausoleum, which had been the intention ... but life was never faithful to any design. There had, for instance, been no moonlit dance at the Taj for Terry and Verita.

Chapter 20

Back at Heathrow Terminal Three, workaholic Verita again bid farewell to Terry, stressing with reasonableness that she was keen to get back to her own flat for a shower before resuming her stint trying to find the two tennis fans who had handed her the box for Javea.

Terry was not a popular scribe when he showed up, unshaven, at the Evening Echo's offices and described how he had been threatened by Karan with death if anything was published about the India expedition. He yearned to get back to Wimbledon, the place where he felt most at ease, and savour the fourth round ties featuring Natalie Sloane and Holly Fleming. But his editor, showing no sympathy for the drama at the Taj, had other ideas. "We need something full of pep for tomorrow's pages," Terry was told. "I'm sending you off to the South of France today, because it's reached my ear that elegant Miss Angela de Jong is filming a television commercial in Cannes. So off you go; get yourself to the InterContinental Carlton on La Croisette by lunchtime. We'll get the stringers to cover Wimbledon."

Many people would have been ecstatic to have an all expenses day trip to Cannes, but Terry wasn't one of them. He wanted to be with Verita, although he acknowledged that that was not possible. As a result, he desired to be at the All England Club, soaking up the atmosphere as the tournament built to its climax, namely the women's singles final on the upcoming Saturday. Wimbledon had been Terry's first love - and a faithful one. The players he'd seen would never understand how they had touched his life and enriched it. If only John McEnroe, who won Wimbledon in 1984, had realised what it meant to the 14 year-young Terry to have bunked off school on 4 July that year, to watch Mac from high up in the old Court No 1 standing area, demolishing journeyman John Sadri in the quarter-finals... But John would never have that awareness of the effect he had on others, because he was always the one being watched, rather than the watcher.

Neither did the stars really grasp why the fans wanted their autographs. That quick scrawl on a bit of paper gave an enthusiast a lifetime's feeling of some type of link, however tenuous, with the player. The signature embodied the experience of the pro up to that moment when pen touched paper. It told the recipient that the celebrity pro had, at least for one or two seconds, recognised the existence of the follower. As one tennis writer (rather more eloquent than Terry) had once stated, such memorabilia would doubtless end up in a glass case in suburbia. But the joy derived in consequence would be anything but transient.

It wasn't hard for Terry to reach Cannes in time. He elected to take a low cost flight from Luton Airport and that took him to Nice in just about one and a half hours. It was a scorching day on the Cote d'Azur and the French palm trees revitalised the newsman's spirits. A taxi soon sped him along the coast to Cannes and the dazzling seafront promenade, La Croisette.

The Carlton hotel loomed large and handsome, overlooking the beautiful blue waves. Terry identified it as the place where Cary Grant had sparred with Grace Kelly in the 1950s Hitchcock film, *To Catch A Thief.* It would be the ideal whereabouts to bring Verita when Javea's murder had been cleared up and Wimbledon was over. Never mind the expense; the luxury would have priceless healing powers for both of them. And for a few days, Terry would take the view that he possessed Cary's legendary charm.

He spotted Angela inside the Carlton, where technicians, arc lights, cameras and sound equipment dominated. To the right of reception, the Bar des Celebrities had become a makeshift dressing room. Angela was in her trademark tennis match clothes, which consisted of a barely-there sleeveless crop top and minimalist, tiny shorts. A make-up artist was brushing the girl's long chestnut hair and reassuring her that she looked awesome. Angela knew Terry from many press conferences and raised her eyebrows as he lumbered in her direction.

Angela's assistant finished combing the superstar's mane and helped her, the main attraction, put on refined, dangling gold earrings, which draped down like sophisticated mini-waterfalls. A male voice shouted to Angela that the first take would be in five minutes. The lackey once again reminded the heroine that she was gorgeous, before moving away and leaving Terry to take his chance. He sat down next to the Dutch princess, and commented: "You're a long way from Wimbledon on your day off. What's happening here?"

"An advertisement. One of my sponsors is a skin cream company. You see, I have no wrinkles and despite sweating in sunlight as part of my job, my skin will always be this smooth. That's what this is all about. The commercial's great. A hot guy chases me through the hotel lobby and I have to run out, cross the road, sprint down the beach and into the water to escape him. All in my tennis gear! Then I emerge from the water, dripping wet but dazzlingly fresh, with my racket in my hand, and I hit a smash, saying: 'Take that! My smash!' Then the guy looks at me, puzzled, and replies: 'I just want to know how my girlfriend can have silky skin like yours; that's all.' So that's when I tell him the name of my skin cream. And that's it: the end of the ad. It's going to be too good, I tell you."

But the facial effervescence dissolved rapidly and Terry could tell that the youngster had more that she wanted to discuss with him. Looking frightened, Angela added quietly: "Jon told me that you know about my relationship with him. Please don't print it, I beg you. I have a very jealous boyfriend who would never forgive me, so I'm putting myself completely in your hands."

"Javea was killed," responded Terry. "Maybe you have information about that. Do you want to share something with me regarding his death?"

"There's nothing to say," replied Angela. "I have only just heard from Jon that he was told by you that Javea saw me leaving Jon's hotel room in Melbourne."

"So you didn't notice that Javea saw you in that hotel corridor? I simply don't believe you. Furthermore, you have another motive to want Javea dead."

"What other motive?"

"The book he was planning."

"I have no knowledge of that."

"Please, Angela, don't infuriate me. Javea informed you that his book would be partly about the flaws in your game."

"He never told me anything."

"Are you certain about that?"

"Yes, I am. Who are you, anyway, to accuse me?"

"Why are you and Smartson an item? Just so that he can side with you on court in difficult moments?"

"Nothing like that, I assure you. I just get lonely when my boyfriend's not travelling with me. I guess I have a thing about older men; older than you, anyway."

"So, who do you think did in Javea?"

"How should I know? I know for a fact that Jon and Karan tried to do something iffy at the time Blanca was playing. Jon had told me Javea was about to publish the details in a book. I'm not going to shield Jon just for the sake of it. Yes, he and Karan could be the murderers, it's definitely possible. And some of us know about Natalie's penchant for drugs. She would kill anyone who was about to let the public into that secret, meaning that - whatever you choose to think - I am not the one responsible for what became of Javea Jackson. I could never kill a good-looking man like him," she concluded with an ignorant half-smile.

"Angela, can we have you now please?" boomed the male voice that Terry had heard earlier. He watched on as Angela rose imperiously and walked right past him without even saying goodbye. The shooting began, and Terry was thankful that he had enough material to write a merry article about the plot for Angela's TV commercial. In Nice airport, he was able to file his story highlighting Angela's burgeoning fame.

Meanwhile, back at Wimbledon, the stringers stepped into the breach without a hitch. Whilst Terry flew to Luton, the Evening Echo became available on the capital's streets. Under a back page banner headline of "SLOANE RANGER!", the paper read:

"NATALIE SLOANE caused a tremendous sensation on Centre Court this afternoon as she battled her way to the quarter-finals with a 6-4, 5-7, 8-6 conquest of glamorous Russian Marina Makarova.

The feisty Brit was locked in combat for 2 hours 39 minutes before edging over the line on her 11th match point with an uncharacteristic serve and volley foray which she completed with an audacious drop volley.

But the staggering quality of the match was overshadowed by an incident in the first set when Miss Sloane pulled ahead 5-4. She had seemed agitated for a number of games but at the changeover she appealed to umpire Ray Fendall whilst pointing her racket to a gentleman in the front row of the seats opposite her.

It transpired that the player had demanded that the male fan, who has not yet been named, should be immediately escorted out of the All England Club.

When Fendall protested that he could not really control impetuous spectators, Miss Sloane snapped: 'Either get him out of here or I'm not playing on. He's been clapping my opponent's unforced errors from the very first point. Either he goes, or I go.'

The tournament referee was summoned to Centre Court whilst the excitable crowd resorted to a slow handclap followed by the customary Mexican wave.

The fiery favourite again insisted that she would default the match to the Russian unless the rowdy spectator was removed. The referee tried to reason with Miss Sloane, but the woman was not to be deterred and she gathered up her racket bag and warm-up jacket.

Only at that point did the referee signal for security guards to forcibly eject the troublesome individual.

The astonishing intervention by Miss Sloane on behalf of her rival shocked the Centre Court and she was even booed after capturing the first set. But by the end of the dramatic tussle many in the stadium had returned their allegiance to the darling of middle England.

In other matches, under-fire No 1 Holly Fleming also made it through to the last eight, amidst rumours that threats have been made on her life. Her father Don conceded: 'It's an excruciatingly enervative time. My daughter is grieving - and now this. But she will not let anyone deter her from her Wimbledon goal.'

There was all sorts of other excitement out on Court No 3 when doubles duo Adele Schmidt and Cristina Gonzales Gomez simultaneously changed their sweat-soaked shirts at the umpire's chair, causing something of a first at Wimbledon. When it last happened, back in 1985, American pro Barbara Potter was embroiled in a singles encounter, and was at least shielded by a resourceful ballboy brandishing a towel. Spurred on by many new-found supporters, Schmidt and Gonzales Gomez ran out winners today."

When Terry saw the piece the following morning, he found himself in agreement with, and admiring of, Natalie's brave stand which had led her to be alienated, at least for some time, from her own devotees. Terry abhorred the recent practice of tennis crowds clapping the mistakes of the players that they wanted to lose. Fine, that was OK for a football match, but tennis had always been of a separate identity by virtue of attracting a less partisan approach. But now the current tennis generation embraced the applauding of double faults, fluffed forehands and mistimed backhands. It just wasn't the same any more. So, in Terry's book, Natalie had acted entirely appropriately. In the final analysis, Wimbledon reserved the right to deny admission to anyone who annoyed the players; it was nice of the Briton to get annoyed on behalf of the girl on the other side of the net.

The rumpus of the previous day inspired Terry to ring around and obtain some quotes so that in about an hour or so he was able to write the following for an early edition of the Echo:

"YOU can call me out of touch, but tennis has been part of me for approximately a quarter of a century.

So I feel I can comment with some authority regarding yesterday's events on Centre Court when our very own Natalie Sloane was the victim of catcalls simply because she bravely came to the aid of an opponent under siege.

We now know that the source of Natalie's discontent was a young Englishman who persistently baited Marina Makarova with loud, protracted and persistent clapping every time the part-time model from Moscow double-faulted or committed an unforced error.

Miss Sloane deserves commendation for demanding that umpire Ray Fendall should deal with the disturbance before play continued. The fact that Miss Sloane had to threaten to walk off court shows just how important she believes court etiquette to be. Without her fit of pique, Miss Makarova may have dissolved early in the second set, thereby denying us an absolute thriller.

It is, accordingly, ironic that Miss Sloane was baited by the very same crowd who loved every second of the 2 hours and 39 minutes' entertainment. They should realise that Natalie came perilously close to disqualification in her bid for justice and a level playing field.

My fellow tennis journalist Chris Singer remarked to me today: 'Natalie was courageous or foolhardy - take your pick. One school of thought will argue that she should have got on and just played her game, but I take your point that she was fighting for something more, an important principle that is woven into the fabric of this great sport.'

And Holly Fleming, who has kept silent ever since her boy-friend Javea Jackson was murdered last Monday, has released a statement through the Women's Tennis Association, saying: 'Whatever our differences, all professional tennis players must applaud the stand taken yesterday by Natalie on behalf of Marina. Wimbledon's own Conditions of Entry state clearly: *'The use of any annoying or dangerous behaviour, foul or abusive language or obscene gestures is forbidden'* and the Club reserves its right to remove from the grounds anyone contravening this, or anyone causing an annoyance or nuisance to any other person. It is there-fore obvious that Wimbledon was wholly correct in its action.'

This isn't the first time something of this nature has occurred in professional tennis. In London's Wembley Arena back in November 1980, John McEnroe was maddened by a female spectator who clapped one of his double faults. The exasper-ated No 1 seed held up play for two minutes, whilst yelling at her: "Who do you think you are?" Umpire Mike Lugg appealed to McEnroe to continue the match - and finally warned him for time delay."

Terry sat back with pride. He hoped Verita would notice his strident masterpiece.

Chapter 21

Terry never made it to the All England Club for the second Tuesday's play, so he only found out many hours later that there had been further singles progress for Jacalyn Jeanice and Angela de Jong, together with another victory for Adele in the doubles.

His editor had expressed satisfaction with the work performed by the lowly stringers, and informed Terry that he would be better utilised securing a one-on-one interview with Holly Fleming. A tip-off to The Echo had said that Holly, disturbed by all the anxiety in her life, was leaving London for the day and would be practising at Frinton-on-Sea.

The reporter reluctantly boarded a train from London's Liverpool Street station, bound for Colchester, and then he would change there to the small branch line which would take him to the quaint, beautiful village of Frinton in Essex. He reckoned it would be about a two-hour journey, followed by a 10-minute walk through majestic, well-kept avenues to the old-fashioned club with its well-manicured grass courts. The clubhouse in Frinton was quintessentially English with its cottage-like exterior and classic thatched roof.

Sure enough he found Holly practising ferociously on the court nearest the charmingly antiquated clubhouse. No other courts were in use and it was incongruous to espy a top player in action in this deserted place. The view was unobstructed by any wire mesh; only a foot high white wall separated Terry from the star. She played a succession of volleys in reply to a constant barrage of vicious shots emanating from the racket of her towering male hitting partner. Her parents were nowhere to be seen; Holly patently wanted to be free of their surveillance. However, unknown to Terry, plained clothes policemen were hiding nearby to both protect the star and to ensure that she made no dash to a domestic airport.

At the end of her session Holly couldn't ignore Terry and in fact came over to ask him: "You wanna talk? Meet me in the bar. I'll just shower." It was that simple for the mild-mannered journalist.

Within 15 minutes they were sitting in luxurious leather seats in the dark wood-panelled bar area. Holly murmured something about her hitting partner having walked up to the village to grab some lunch. "I'm in a lot of trouble," started Holly. "Last Monday I was focussed on winning Wimbledon and getting married next month. Now, my fiancé is killed and I don't care if I win Wimbledon. I have had to give my fingerprints and, OK, so have others. But I am also suffering death threats and, if I'm not mistaken, I'm going to be arrested for my fiancé's murder as soon as my Wimbledon ceases. Do you think it can get any worse than this, Mr Proudley?"

Terry regarded the diminutive phenomenon and noticed a cluster of pimples on what used to be her unblemished face. Her lips looked dry and in bad shape, and there was a tinge of red, and regret, in the eyes. She was still ravishing, but the usual sparkle was missing.

"I won't lie to you, Holly. It does indeed look very bad for you. The theorists will claim that you must have poisoned Javea as a reaction to the newspapers saying he had been intimate with Larissa LaDame. Many people think you had the most obvious reason to see him dead."

"Not only that," replied Holly. "My fingerprints were found on a jar of marmalade at Jav's place. That's not untrue; I brought him marmalade last Monday morning. But my parents have been told that the marmalade jar carrying my prints was contaminated with rat poison. But how can I prove that I had no idea it was poisoned?"

"You must have spoken to Javea when you brought the marmalade to him. Had you seen the Larissa story at that time?"

"I can tell where you're heading. You think I killed him, too, and that I did it deliberately and in cold blood once the Larissa thing was in the paper. The odds are totally stacked against my surviving this. My parents have also been told that there was another jar of poisoned marmalade without prints. At first I thought this would be my lifeline, and that I could prove my innocence. And then the thought hit me: the police will simply think I plotted for there to be two jars to be twice as definite that Javea was murdered. So how can I emerge from all this? Perhaps I should win Wimbledon and then kill myself, to be out of this terrible hole."

Holly then burst into tears and Terry had to hug the sobbing girl as she fell forward into his arms. "I can't go on," she wailed, "why can't Javea still be alive to prove my innocence? How could Larissa do this to me? She's stolen my Javea and my life and now I'm going to pay with my entire existence. I hate her, I hate her so much. Why can't she be dead, instead of me!"

The jagged crying fit stopped abruptly and Holly looked fixedly at the wood panelling around her. After a pause, Terry asked: "Did you know Javea planned to write about your tennis, and how perhaps to beat you, in a book?"

"That never bothered me," asserted Holly. "If I'm better than the rest, I'm better than the rest. I wouldn't want to be No 1 and have it doubted. I have no fear of healthy competition on court. If Stan Power wanted it this way, then I would never impede that, and it was never an issue between me and Jav, never."

"Do you draw any comfort from fan mail at this time?" asked Terry. "I mean, things are mighty tough, so does that divert your mind and give you any solace at all?"

"I never read it," said Holly. "Who knows who the people are, writing to you. They could all be crackers! I just sign postcards from time to time and my parents handle all that stuff. The only time I feel calm is when I'm on court; it's like a parallel universe for me where I'm in control and no-one can get at me and I'm free to be serious and craft out a victory. It's the only time I truly respect myself, to be honest. My self-worth is bound up inside the baseline. Ah, there's a good quote for you!"

"Is there anything I can write that can help you? My editor sent me here to see how a highly pressured sportswoman can possibly function when accused of murder and under death threats. How do you do it?"

"Like I said, write a piece for me which praises my strength of character! Tell the world that I'm a fighter and won't give up. If I get through all this I'll be tougher and wiser. Like I think Greg Rusedski once said, whatever doesn't kill you, makes you stronger. That's my style at the moment. So long as I am found innocent of Jav's murder, I will survive."

It was a good time for Terry to take his leave. His subsequent article paid tribute to Holly Fleming's indefatigability and endurance, whilst skimming over the rumours alleging she was responsible for Jackson's demise. But on the train home, it occurred to Terry that he was no closer to knowing whether or not Holly was the killer.

Chapter 22

By Wednesday, uniformed Verita was looking far more relaxed at the All England Club and seemed thoroughly self-assured as she moved through the tournament grounds. She had agreed to meet Terry at 11am at the Court 11 cafe to update him on the official investigation.

"It's been too long," she said, with a smile, as she sat down next to the newsman. "I'm sorry I'm a few minutes late."

"You look, er, really marvellous," said Terry.

"Well, thank you," beamed Verita. "I'm so sorry I'm one of those sad cases whose mood is determined by what's happening in my professional life. Things are a lot clearer today, thank God."

"Why? What's been developing?"

"We had a stroke of immense luck. One guy and one woman basically voluntarily came forward and gave themselves up for questioning. It seems that they were frightened at first, but ultimately decided to talk to us."

"Who are they?"

"The couple who handed me the box at Rectory Orchard to go to Javea Jackson. I never thought we would find them, but I'm so pleased we did. My superior officer and I interviewed each of them yesterday."

"And what transpired?"

"They admitted that they were the young couple, both wearing sunglasses and dark hooded tops, who came up to me when I was on duty last Monday at the entrance to Rectory Orchard. They stated that they had handed me a box which they hoped would be put before Javea."

"Meaning?"

"Nothing confessional. They told us that they are both from Amsterdam and unofficially produced a newsletter from time to time chronicling the latest titbits of Jackson's globe-trotting life. People knew from one of the newsletters that this pair would be travelling to Wimbledon, and that's when the marmalade started being sent to these two, for onward transmission to the British hero."

"It seems that the circulation of this newsletter is an issue worth looking at."

"Of course, but they've already told us something vital - that they sent copies of it, care of tournaments and national tennis associations, to all the sport's big names, including Drew Todd, Jon Smartson, and Jacalyn, Adele, Holly, Natalie and Angela. They wanted to impress these people and also see if one day they might become celebrity contributors to future newsletters."

"How does this make you feel?"

"My superior is as convinced as I am that these two are blameless and had absolutely no idea that they were carrying poisoned marmalade to their hero. Each of them is in horrific shock and they even offered to have their homes back in Holland raided by police, and so on. The situation is this. Holly must have wanted to destroy Jackson because she firmly believed he cheated on her - and someone else on the tennis circuit must have had another, equally significant reason to poison him. We still don't know which of the two, differing rat-poisoned marmalades caused the death, but Holly is on the hook for attempted murder, if nothing more."

"Did you see my piece in the paper about Holly?"

"'My self-worth is bound up inside the baseline.' What is all that about? You're too sentimental, Terry, far too sentimental. I mean, you wrote the thing beautifully, with style and panache. It was very moving. But I've noticed you like to back the underdog.

It's like, I also saw your article about Natalie Sloane and how sorry you felt for her because the crowds trashed her. Don't get me wrong: you're a sweetheart, my sweetheart. I hope you'll be writing a magnificent feature in a few days' time about how WPC Verita Sassi brought the killer to justice!"

"Let's hope so; and who will it be, anyway?"

"It's too early to tell, isn't it, but would you want to be Holly Fleming right now?"

"Definitely not, but somehow I hope it isn't her. Let it be someone such as…"

"Terry, my dearest. Stop dreaming. I have to go. Ironically I'm one of those who have to guard Holly Fleming today against those death threats."

"Take greatest care."

"Surely."

After Verita's departure from him, Terry closed his eyes in meditative contemplation. But in a matter of minutes Larissa La Dame prodded his shoulder and made for the seat which had been Verita's.

"Well, Mr Proudley, the offers are already flooding in. Whoever said that notoriety doesn't pay? I'm inundated with work opportunities. Music, stage, film, TV, ads. You name it, everyone wants me. There may even be a mini-serial about Javea's death in America. I think I'm made for life! And as for Holly, she's a murderer, isn't she?"

"Are you here to gloat?" bristled Proudley. "You're so proud of your good fortune arising out of the saddest of events. How can you live with yourself?"

"Easily. It's not my fault I'm not the killer, even though people like you wish I was. But I'll tell you something I didn't tell the police. Y'know what? They are very easy to lie to. I told them I was nowhere near the road where Jav was when he died, but - between you and me - I was walking past that Rectory Orchard no-through street, probably around the time of the murder. But I'm not the one who did it, so don't get any ideas."

"I don't want to know any of this," retorted Terry. "I am not a police officer. I thought I could maybe find out the murderer, but this is all too complicated for me. All I know about is tennis, and that's the way it's going to stay."

"Yeah, well I'm not telling the police where I was, and if you did, I'll kill you!" exclaimed Larissa.

They stared at each other for a few unpleasant seconds; Larissa then stormed off, her face like thunder. Terry's nerves were shot through. He decided to not even tell Verita about his latest confrontation with Larissa. Tennis was far more leisurely than fighting crime.

The writer now wished that he knew nothing about Javea Jackson, and nothing about his death or the suspects. He wanted a simple life where he had tennis and Verita: nothing more. He could see that the inquiry was exhausting Verita and now he wanted the whole thing to stop. Deep down it scared him that the killer might come after him. It therefore would be good not to know too much, if that was still possible. It sounded cowardly but the investigation was in the hands of WPC Sassi's superiors; it was not his responsibility.

Terry perked himself up by dreaming of the long holiday he and Verita would take once the crime was solved. He lapped up hopes of glorious days full of fun, sun and blissful togetherness. It calmed him to see so many happy couples walking around Wimbledon, and he imagined drinking champagne with his lady love in the tournament long bar, if only Javea's executioner could be caught speedily.

Chapter 23

From the Court 11 cafe, Terry Proudley walked in the direction of the green canvas backstop of Court No 6 and then passed the spot where he had spoken a few days earlier with Drew Todd, and from there he strode on, with the west stand of Court No 2 to his right. At Gate 13 he happened to meet Natalie Sloane entering the grounds to his left, amongst a phalanx of security guards. They were keeping at bay thrilled fans brandishing cameras and pens for an autograph. She wore a baggy pale blue sweatshirt and black tracksuit trousers; neither flattered her. Over her left shoulder she carried a gigantic racquet bag.

The petite, slightly ordinary player grinned at Terry and shouted: "Come this way! I want to talk to you in the competitors' complex!"

The reporter dutifully tagged along besides the stern guards as they all marched up the slight incline where the general public were forbidden to tread. The watchmen left Natalie at the competitors' entrance, and she looked back at Terry, crying: "Come on! I'll get you in."

Terry diffidently followed, and the staff at the front desk smiled with appreciation at Natalie, who breezily commented: "He's with me! I'll sign for him later."

Together, they mounted the spiral staircase to the bright, modern players' restaurant, which looked onto the outside courts on the other side of the south concourse. Natalie ignored the other players and signalled Terry to a quiet corner of the restaurant, which had a very clear view of Court No 2.

She flung down the racket bag, and pulled up two chairs so that they could sit with their backs to everyone and pretend that Court No 2 was the centre of their attention.

"I don't know you well," began Natalie purposefully, "but it's noticeable to me that you're often with that police lady. Can't really blame you, she looks great. But anyway, you also know tennis nearly as well as me. I was wide awake last night thinking of you, and then Javea, me, my tennis, this situation and I decided I wanted to talk to you. And the real reason is because I want to turn over a new leaf and, at the same time, give my view on who might have taken Javea's life."

"What suddenly makes you so keen to express yourself?"

"I guess, because I'm guilty about who I am. Some of my rivals know that I've dabbled in drugs during my off-season, and I won't deny it to you. I believe that you are a man of integrity and won't publish anything about it, because I can tell you have a sensitive side and want to believe people will live up to your own standards."

"Thanks for the compliment. I'm too soft, it's true. You're the best woman player this country has; it would depress me to destroy you. Are you saying that drugs didn't help your performance?"

"I took cocaine to escape, Terry. To escape from feeling socially awkward, to escape the tension brought on by matches, and the misery of always making your happiness wait to the future and be dependent on success at this wretched game. I regret it; I have let myself down. But the cocaine ruined my concentration and the doctors I've seen privately to break the habit have all told me that this addiction undermines my performance. So I doubt many of the girls care if I continued to run myself into the ground. It would just mean one less person to have to beat to reach the top."

"Have you any idea who the assassin might be?"

"I think so, yes. Javea told me in Paris about the book he was going to do, telling everyone how to defeat me, Jacalyn, Holly and Angela. It annoyed me, but then I thought well, it's the same for all of us, so I should just let it happen and allow the whole thing to wash over me. But in the same conversation he confidentially explained to me that Angela and Jon Smartson were having an affair and that it would be in my interests to try to veto Smartson as umpire for any match I played against Angela. According to Javea, Angela had reacted badly when he told her about the prospective book and that he knew she was having a thing with Smartson. At the time I found it really funny, but now…"

"Javea told you he'd already spoken to Angela about the book and his knowledge of her affair with Smartson. Are you totally sure of that?"

"Yes, that's right. But you don't realise that Angela's boyfriend is way too possessive and jealous. He could turn really aggressive, I suspect, if he knew how she really behaves when he's not with the tour."

"That's one interpretation," murmured Terry.

"From what Javea said to me, you could equally argue that Smartson is the one with no morals, couldn't you."

"True. You don't like either of them, do you?"

"There's no reason why I should. If you ask me, Smartson and Angela are the joint killers of Javea Jackson. I just hope the police will find it out before anyone else gets hurt."

"Do you think that another murder is likely?"

"You can never tell, can you, but I think it's definitely on the cards with such heartless people running around here. If Wimbledon wasn't my own country's event, I would have been out of here before now like a shot."

"What would you say if I told you some people suspect you, Natalie? You're hardly whiter than white. If Javea had written about your cocaine in his biography, all your sponsorships would have ended abruptly. All of the sponsors would have relied on contractual clauses saying that you mustn't bring them into disrepute."

"I won't lie to you. Javea was at a party and saw me snorting coke. He wouldn't have approved, I'm sure. But an abuser of drugs is not necessarily a murderer. I knew he was an outspoken bloke who could pull the pin on me at any time, but I didn't poison him, I swear. But this brush with death has completely got to me. I'm going to go clean now, believe me Terry - I want you to be the first to know the new Natalie Sloane."

"It sounds admirable, it really does. But I have to keep my journalistic distance. So I'll wish you well, but I can't say much more than that. You've got to straighten yourself out, or else you'll end up dead."

"That wouldn't be a good double whammy for British tennis," remarked the player, trying to break the serious atmosphere.

"Tell me," ventured Terry, "what do you think was the weakness in your game that Javea would have written in his book?"

"Oh, that's easy," smiled Natalie. "I'm hopeless if someone plays it wide to my forehand, I just can't get into position in time and I lose the point pretty quickly. Thankfully for me, no-one but Stan Power ever seems to notice."

"I think I do," said Terry. "But a gentleman doesn't seek to inflict pain. Good luck today in your quarter-final. I'm a little patriotic, after all."

"You know, you really are a remarkable man," said Natalie. "It's a shame there aren't more Terry Proudleys in the world."

"And more Natalie Sloanes to note his true worth," replied Terry wryly.

It was only later that Terry recalled Karan saying that Natalie had been "furious" when she found out Javea planned to detail her tennis blemishes. Terry kicked himself for having let that fact slip from his memory.

Chapter 24

The British press and TV stations had been constantly speculating about Natalie's chances of winning the tournament, ever since the initial shock of Javea's death had faded a little. The nation seemed to believe that the impact of Jackson's demise could somehow be lessened if only Natalie could triumph on the Centre Court.

Everyone wanted a piece of Natalie. Photographers camped outside her Wimbledon home, and they were also waiting outside any restaurant she frequented in the evenings, perhaps tipped off by the waiters, who themselves wanted her autograph. She had no idea how anyone had got hold of the numbers for her landline and mobile, but both rang off the hook and she had to jettison them in order to stay composed.

If she turned on the television, she came face to face with a pundit saying how he couldn't believe she could hold her racket, given all the fuss about her sweeping the country. Luckily, she never gave any thought to her compatriots' hopes for her, realising that if she did, she would become a bundle of nerves collapsing on court in front of the royal box.

She resented the fact that she lacked Holly's exquisite form. If only I was taller, slimmer and had a voice which drove men crazy, sighed Natalie. But it was her deficits that had motivated her to make something of herself, and another three wins would see her become Wimbledon Champion.

Perhaps, if that happened, the section of the public that had slated her soon after Javea died would make their peace. The media had really rebuked her for what she'd said in that press conference: "Personally I don't care about any other player but myself." Her coach had tried to limit the damage by arguing on Radio Five Live: "It wasn't meant to have been a disrespectful dismissal of Javea; the statement has been taken out of context because Natalie's intent had been to emphasise that tennis would still please people, as the game is always being renewed with fresh combatants who are capable of being entertainers." But there followed letters to the papers, coupled with editorials and feature columns, all maintaining that Natalie's comments mirrored declining nationwide moral standards amongst the young. That reaction, in turn, predictably caused some rebellious adolescents at the All England Club to become vociferous and vocal in their support of her.

Within a day or two the row had virtually disappeared, because Britain's sports lovers had a feeling that Natalie might just win the whole thing. They wanted to be part of the ecstasy of success if she did, and, therefore, forgiving her for being outspoken and professionally ruthless was the best option. But deep down her coach had no idea whether or not his pupil was a murderer and his uncertainty was heightened by the knowledge that Natalie appeared to have had some sort of quiet passion for handsome Javea, which of course had been at violent odds with how the man himself thought about her.

On Centre Court Natalie told herself to disregard completely any negative emotions and forget her worry and the prurient crowd. The aim was to play a flawless game against Japan's Eriko Tanaka. There was no point trying to win for her parents, who had little interest in tennis. The strategy was to attain success for her own happiness.

The trick was to ignore any temporary setback during the match, and remain totally of the conviction that Tanaka would lose. "I am the best, I am the best," chanted Natalie under her breath in between points and when changing ends. She stayed determined to hit each shot sweetly, as if it were her last. With the help of mental imagery, the Briton slammed in tough first serves and bent her knees into position for each ground stroke. Natalie kept her eyes tracking the yellow fuzzy ball at all times and hit it on each occasion with the determination that it should not come back again. At last the global plan paid off, and with Centre Court erupting in elation, Natalie understood that she had moved into the semi-finals.

Holly Fleming also overcame her quarter-final opponent, but once again it seemed as if her mind was elsewhere as she made strange errors and prevailed unconvincingly. The audience was quiet and almost numb, no doubt mulling over the death threats that were ongoing against Miss Fleming, together with the rumours that she may have eliminated her fiancé.

Adele Schmidt and Cristina Gonzalez Gomez received the biggest cheer of the day when they once more changed their shirts at a changeover - this time by the umpire's chair on Court No 1. Cameras whirred excitedly and they received a slightly tongue-in-cheek standing ovation when they took their first match point - which put them into the ladies' doubles final.

"This means everything to me," Adele told the Austrian reporters. "This is why you play the sport - for days like these. I am too happy to speak. Today I know for certain that my name will always be up there in gilt letters on the boards at Wimbledon proclaiming each year's winners and runners-up. But I want to make sure I win - that is really my entire life's ambition."

Terry tried to absorb the day's tennis, but found his attention thwarted by a reassessment of the murder suspects.

Drew Todd had every reason to be the killer. As soon as everyone knew he was a racist, all the sports goods companies would run a mile from him. Larissa LaDame looked to be on the brink of making big money out of Javea, so the death had proven beneficial for her. Then there was Angela de Jong. What would have become of her if Javea had written that she gave the officials certain favours in the hope of protection on court? And what about Natalie? Her endorsements would be gone if the cocaine tales went into print. As for Holly, well, her prints were at the murder scene and she had a strong motive in view of the Larissa newspaper exposé. Adele Schmidt had publicly said she wanted to kill Javea, and Karan and Blanca had an obvious incentive due to the scam. As did Smartson, especially thanks to his association with Angela.

Terry questioned whether the police were any further forward at all. Would they really arrest Holly in a day or two's time? How would the investigation progress once all the main suspects left the country at the end of the event? In the meantime, he had to file his story, and hope for the best.

Chapter 25

Thursday at Wimbledon was supposed to see Jacalyn Jeanice and Angela de Jong in last eight action, gunning for semi-finals places against each other on Friday, with the ladies' singles final scheduled for Saturday. The scrapping of the men's event, owing to Javea's demise, meant that everything was due to finish one day earlier than planned, because there would be no men's final on Sunday.

But someone somewhere was tenaciously undermining the revised programme at the All England Club. It was just about midday when a cleaner, undertaking an hourly inspection of the toilets in the club's museum opposite Court No 17, found a woman slumped in one of the cubicles. It was too early in the day for anyone to be drunk. And then the bullet wound at the right temple told its own story. Larissa LaDame was dead, having been shot in cold blood.

The police responded by evacuating the museum and the Wimbledon shop which neighboured it. The tea lawn area was the next to be cleared. But soon there was a risk of rising panic amongst the fans. In consequence, the club chairman, having held an urgent crisis meeting with his committee of management and the rest of the tournament executive, made a tannoy announcement that the day's play was now cancelled. He kept repeating the fact that all tickets would be refunded and as news spread around the venue that another Wimbledon murder had taken place, most people were swift to depart for their homes.

Terry holed himself up in the Wimbledon press bar and quietly looked back on his notes about Larissa. It seemed so long ago since Javea had sent that email, admitting that he'd seen LaDame at various social functions, and adding that she was basically trying to extort money from him against threats of increasingly intimate revelations to the papers. And Javea had said - whether it was true or not - that he hadn't cheated on Holly.

On the other hand, when Terry had had that discussion with the tantalising femme fatale at Cafe Pergola, she'd been at pains to point out that, in her view at least, she had successfully stolen Javea away from Holly. She'd patently been physically attracted to Jackson, but her satisfaction seemed to stem chiefly from her observation: "I can sell my story cos I was with a living legend ... only he's not living now, but that makes my story all the more valuable."

Larissa's death seemed to point once again to Holly Fleming. There was no other reason for any of the other suspects to feel deep-rooted hostility towards her. As Terry pondered the situation, he couldn't help but overhear some of his colleagues drinking in a group, with their chatter referring to whispers already emerging that Holly had been seen earlier, near the time of Larissa's death, walking alone in her trademark all-white tracksuit near Court No 17 and Gate 4, thereby close to the museum.

Then Terry recalled that when he last spoke with Larissa, the latter was publicly labelling Holly the killer, whilst also boasting that she was making a great deal of money from the cessation of Jackson. The provocation had been colossal, and Terry could see how Holly could have been pushed mentally over the edge. He knew that Holly had been deeply in love with Britain's great young tennis star.

The noise levels rose in the press bar and the increasing cigarette smoke began to irritate Terry. He could only see Holly as the destroyer of Larissa, and it disappointed him. He admired Holly, and all that the youngster had achieved, and now she'd gone and thrown it all away.

The journalist left the press bar and was surprised to find it was raining as he emerged onto the south concourse by Court

No 2. He wandered aimlessly about the outer courts, all covered by green tarpaulins that billowed thanks to the hot air blowing beneath them, which was being mechanically pumped onto the court surface. The clouds were granite grey above, whilst wind whistled in the trees. Raindrops refreshed Terry's face, but all he wanted was Verita, and only she could soothe him.

Out of the blue WPC Sassi was straight ahead of Terry as he approached the Wimbledon Shop by Gate 4. The glamorous beauty smiled affectionately, before saying: "It's brilliant to see you. My fear ebbs away when I'm with you."

"It looks like Holly has no escape this time."

"I agree. She was seen just over there, near Court 17, just a few minutes before poor Larissa must have been shot. She's denying everything, of course, but there's no-one else who wanted to see the back of Larissa, although Javea might have been tempted if he was still alive. No doubt she got him in loads of trouble with Holly."

"So what happens now?"

"Actually, the whole thing's a pain. They're going to let Holly play on in the tournament until she wins or gets beaten. That, in turn, causes a logistical nightmare cos there are continuous, anonymous death threats against her, and people like me have to constantly protect her. It's becoming farcical because police resources are being diverted away from the murder enquiry, simply because Ms Fleming keeps on winning."

"What's the answer?"

"Actually, the police plan now is to seize the passports of all the suspects before the end of the tournament; that way we can restrain them all here and do all the necessary questioning. Well, let's put it this way, we'll invite all the suspects to give up their passports and only someone very foolish will intimate that they have a burning need to flee the country. If they play it that way, they'll be followed and won't have a moment's peace or privacy."

"But isn't it true to say that they're bound to co-operate now that it seems Holly will soon be charged with two murders? Isn't it just a case of some last-minute evidential eliminations and then they'll all be on their way, except Holly?"

"I think you're right, because my belief is that Holly is responsible for both jars of poisoned marmalade. Maybe she planned for a long time to kill Jackson, if she had an inkling he was being unfaithful. I think she kept up appearances for a while - and then struck."

"It's very sad," pronounced Terry, "that it was the errors in others that took Holly down the path of retribution. If only those around her hadn't upset her so much."

"Don't worry. When all this is over, there will still be you and me, and nothing is more important than that."

Chapter 26

Ticket-holders for Wimbledon's second Friday were not deterred by the murder of Larissa LaDame. The consensus opinion was that the shooting had to be inextricably linked with the poisoning of Javea, and so the majority smugly entered the All England Club, enthusiastic about the tennis on offer, which had been brought forward to begin at 11am.

First up on Centre Court would be Adele Schmidt and Cristina Gonazalez Gomez in the women's doubles final, followed by Natalie Sloane against Holly Fleming. The third fixture on Centre would involve the winner of the two remaining quarter-finals, which would start on Courts No 1 and No 2 at 11am.

It could have been a result of arrogance, but both Jacalyn and Angela considered themselves fitter than the other, and they had therefore both agreed to play their quarters and, potentially, semi on the same day.

The papers that had gone to print overnight had somehow heard that Holly was due to be arrested and charged with two murders by Saturday early evening at the latest, once the women's singles final was over. The same papers were deeply critical of the police's willingness to stand back and watch until Holly stopped playing in the tournament. Their pages appeared to be a patriotic frenzy designed to catapult Natalie into the final.

Adele Schmidt practised with Cristina on Court No 4 before their date with destiny on Centre Court. Under overcast skies, Terry watched as the two girls moved gingerly on the damp grass, and he was amused to see that they both wore short white T-shirts emblazoned in black italics with the word "Treasure". The tops revealed, in de rigeur fashion, their tanned midriffs, and their skirts were silky white and skin-tight. It was a mystery to Terry as to how they actually managed to move when dressed like that.

The two girls were soon slipping and sliding as they took it in turns to play serve and volley, and the fans around the court felt the chill as a fine drizzle developed. Two minutes later the spitting rain transformed into a cloudburst and the players quickly packed up their things and covered their heads with towels as they made for the locker-room, oblivious to spectators seeking impromptu signatures.

Another 30 minutes of steady downpour had dampened Wimbledon when Adele, anxious to rid herself of nerves, walked into the Court No 1 stadium and chanced to find Terry alone, his hands in a light overcoat, sitting and watching the deluge. Both of them were used to rain breaks in London SW19, but only Terry enjoyed them. The curvy athlete took the seat next to him.

"I like it here," he said to Adele's unspoken question. "Rain is romantic, don't you think? I can rest here and reflect on what's going on in my life."

"So what is going on?" asked Adele.

"Perhaps my life is about to become very exciting, and yet I don't think you should place your happiness in the hands of others. They may disappoint you. But at the moment my soul is full of love and I see sunshine and no stress in my near future, if the murderer is first apprehended."

"I want a holiday, too," said the blonde. "But before that, Cristina and I must take our title. Then my life will be complete."

"Is success more significant to you than love?"

"Definitely, because a success is always with you, and never leaves. Lovers come and go, so for me success is my key to being happy."

"You've wanted a Grand Slam for so long, right?"

"Right; all my living memories involve the hope of this title and now it's finally in my grasp. They'll build a marble sculpture of me in my home town if I can only do the business today."

"Did you know that some are saying you have declared you wanted to kill Javea Jackson?"

"Anyone could have killed him, in truth. Am I one of them? Yes. Did I think about doing it? Oh yes, it more than crossed my mind. Jackson thought he was better than us. I don't care he's gone because he did me wrong and belittled me. But I'm too clever to get stuck in trouble. He tried to prevent me from fulfilling my life's desire, and I hated him for that stunt he pulled, but it's obvious now that Holly thought she had a much stronger rationale to strike him down. Let's face it, everyone's saying it was Holly, so trust me, it was Holly."

"Will you win today?"

"If these floods subside, we'll do it today. If they don't, you'll see us win tomorrow."

Adele's prediction turned out to be spot-on. Later that afternoon, once the cold winds blew away the heaviest of the clouds, she and Cristina torpedoed their adversaries and hugged and kissed each other in celebration of their accomplishment live on TV before the prize ceremony.

Natalie Sloane then endeavoured to fit Britain's new characterisation of her as righteous heroine, but the occasion was too much for her, and she broke down in tears having lost to Holly, who consoled the No 4 seed with calming words as they left Centre Court together. Some of the Union Jack flag-wavers had booed the American when she stepped out at the commencement of the semi-final, and there was only a smattering of applause to greet her victory. The stands simply didn't want to show any backing for the police's principal suspect.

What the masses had no idea about was that Holly was falling in love and the experience had infused her entire being with unexpected, but very welcome, harmony. The object of her affections was none other than Terry Proudley. Holly felt that her life was nearing its end, and that she had wasted her sensitive side on a self-loving athlete. In Terry she saw a real man, with real emotions and a sense of humour and a real willingness to care for others. He was more intelligent than Javea had been, and she liked that, too. The man was a writer after all - that was cool. She felt aroused when he had held her whilst she cried at the tennis club and the article he'd created the next day had been so admiring without being at all obsequious or creepy. The thought of one day having Terry was sustaining her in her darkest moments. True, he was a bit fat if she was perfectly honest, but they could sweat that out together, if they ever had the opportunity. It was too bad that daily she was fighting her sense that all was lost. She actually felt too low to communicate her feelings to Terry. Besides, he seemed to think - in the final analysis - that she was guilty, so what was the point? And she'd heard the stories that he was perpetually gooey-eyed for the sultry policewoman who kept showing up at Wimbledon.

So there was only one thing for Holly to do - watch the second semi-final, which, courtesy of results earlier in the day, had duly lined up Jacalyn Jeanice versus Angela de Jong.

Chapter 27

The lanky Dutch world No 2 looked cool and composed as the second semi-final got under way on Centre Court, with Holly scrutinising every stroke from the stands. Yet internally, the haughty luminary from Amsterdam was badly shaken. Jon Smartson had told her the night before that the Wimbledon chiefs had informed him he would be the umpire for the ladies' singles final. That was what she had hoped for, and banked on, because he was a senior official and was the most likely candidate for the job this year.

But Smartson hadn't been pleased because the gossip he'd heard was that Karan had used some duress on some of the denizens of the All England Club to make totally sure of the appointment. Smartson had been angry because he now believed that Karan carried a torch for Angela and his conclusion was that Karan was now Angela's second choice, behind her volatile boyfriend, with himself destined to be cut adrift as a lowly (or non-existent) No 3.

Angela reflected on the fact that she had been seeing Karan from time to time in the recent past, but she believed their trysts had been completely clandestine because she had been extremely careful to keep the whole affair under wraps. She worried that Smartson may now take revenge if she made it to the final and she also felt furious with Karan for interfering and causing the whole dilemma.

Angela dropped her opening two service games and, trailing 0-3, stared across the net at pretty Jacalyn who was preparing to serve. Just as the French pin-up was well into her service motion and about to connect with the ball at its apogee, there was some commotion in the seats to Angela's right-hand side. The ethereal Miss de Jong peered upwards at the sea of faces and almost fainted as she saw Karan belatedly taking a seat, next to Drew Todd of all people. So he was actually here, in London. That was appalling; it would only make matters worse!

The Amsterdam belle looked back at Jacalyn and made a desperate effort to direct her mind back to the game. Little did she know that Verita and her senior colleagues were, at that very moment, celebrating their successful bid to lure Karan from India to England, where they could monitor him close-up. It hadn't been difficult; they'd fooled the star's secretary that there was to be an awards ceremony in London that evening (which would be taped and then broadcast at a later date) with huge appearance money for Karan. All he had to do was turn up and be feted. The headstrong personality had fallen for the plan hook, line and sinker and had taken the view he'd be fine getting in and out of the country by travelling on a false passport. But he'd succeeded in trapping himself.

3-0 rapidly became 5-0 before Angela decided to stop the rot. She started belting the ball from sideline to sideline and Jacalyn, though fleet of foot, was nonetheless immediately at full stretch. At 1-5, when the Parisien raced across court, but only in vain, as a de Jong winner flashed past her, the teenager threw her racket to a startled ballboy who instantaneously tried to pass it straight back.

Jacalyn had other ideas: she ushered him to the baseline and, with the racket still in his hand, she intimated that he should play the next point. Angela glowered for a moment before realising that she would be branded a sour spoilsport if she didn't participate willingly in the charade. So the leggy big shot hit a serve to the ballboy and, all credit to him, he returned the ball sweetly - much to the delight of the crowd. Angela obediently traded a few shots with the kid and then suddenly - to everyone's wonder - the ballboy hit a professional-looking backhand slice approach shot. Angela tried to rip a winner past him, but he bolted up to the net and hit a most beautiful backhand angled drop volley to capture the point! De Jong flung her racket to the ground, but the roaring fans were already standing and clapping enthusiastically. Jacalyn broke into spontaneous giggles.

The red-faced stripling meekly ran back, mortified, to his peripheral position, but he had already become part of Wimbledon folklore. Angela's first set fight-back was sunk by the incident, and in a twinkling of an eye it was 6-1, Jeanice.

In the second set Miss Jeanice lost concentration. Her brain filled with memories of Javea and she looked back on what she could have done differently to net him as her lover. At times she remained tender towards him, but there had also been, and still were, days of blind rage. As the points against Angela came and went, she adjudged that she had really always hated him, ever since his first needless rejection of her. She abhorred Javea for scarring irrevocably her whole life. His death was indeed an emancipation.

Jacalyn's mental anguish allowed Angela to level at one set all: it had been 6-3, de Jong.

The final set was intoxicating and stimulating. Jacalyn jumped ahead 4-0, but wily Angela stuck to her task and punched the air as she accrued point by point in a patient climb to 4-4. Both girls were bathed in sweat as they tussled for a sliver of superiority, but there can only be one winner in tennis, and the slender, long-limbed fighter Angela de Jong held on grimly to overcome sylphlike Jacalyn Jeanice, 8-6. The victor slumped to her knees on the dusty baseline, and the loser dragged herself slowly to the net for what would be the briefest of handshakes between the two of them.

Nonetheless, with a super-human effort, Jacalyn clapped her racket against her hand in appreciation of all four sides of the stadium, and everyone was euphoric when she once again hit pre-signed tennis balls to acknowledge her faithful supporters.

Events moved fast after the semi-final. The police arrested Karan as he was leaving the club, based on allegations of coercion, which were well-founded as the Wimbledon officials threatened by Karan had been wired for sound. None of the other individuals under suspicion were arranging to leave the country, as they all made clear to the chief inspector in their own idiosyncratic ways. The perception was that Holly's arrest was imminent and then they'd soon be on their way. None of them relished the alternative of being under 24-hour surveillance overseas.

For Holly Fleming, it seemed as if nothing would matter once another 24 hours had elapsed. She wanted Terry, but her discreet enquiries confirmed that he had a serious interest in the policewoman who looked so fantastic. So the only thing left to do was to beat Angela and smile in front of all the cameramen and then hope that everything would fade to black. In her heart of hearts, the prodigy knew that she couldn't break free and it was useless to hold onto any shred of hope. Tomorrow she was bound to lose, even if she won. She would miss the adulation, the attention, the press conferences, the prizes, the riches and the drama - but all good things had to come to an end.

Chapter 28

Terry had few friends because he disliked social gatherings. He detested meeting new people, introducing himself, making himself sound interesting, and sounding interested in others ... it was a chore and a bore. He encountered very few people who he could gel with, and found it especially hard to make male friends. But he would always have time for his former law school pal, Marcus Jones.

Marcus had sensed Terry's pain at having to be in law school, and actively persuaded his fellow student to dare to be himself and seek what he truly coveted. When Terry had been all at sea and despondent, Marcus had inspired him and firmly advised him to forget law and put all his time and energy into aiming to be a sports writer. For that loyalty and optimistic fervour, Terry would forever be thankful. He had been heading for oblivion and good old Marcus had been the ballast that saved him from drowning.

They now saw each other far too infrequently, but were always there for each other whenever there was good news to be shared, or sadness attributable to girlfriend troubles or professional woes. Terry had seen Marcus' text message at the end of Holly's match and, though it would have been simple to feign tiredness, he replied straight away, offering to catch up with Marcus at the Dog & Fox pub in Wimbledon Village. Marcus was an accommodating type, so Terry already knew that they would have a quick drink before heading over the road to the Indian restaurant, Rajdoot, on the corner.

The journalist smiled inwardly as Marcus, tall, thin and intellectual, bustled into the public house about 20 minutes late, with his eyes darting right and left to locate his long-term ally. Terry went up to him to save the guy's embarrassment and they both ordered lagers and stood at the bar.

"I'm sorry I'm late," said Marcus, "but it's hell at work at the moment. You know, there's no let-up. As soon as I try to settle on one file, either my boss delegates some more of his stuff to me, or else the clients themselves ring up to give me new instructions. It's a nightmare."

"Your problem is you can't say no."

"As a lawyer you can never say no. Even when you're really overstretched, if you miss a deadline, that's it, you can be sued for negligence and get struck off. I try to work as quickly as possible, but how can you read mounds of paperwork about a complex 24 million dollars construction claim very quickly? It's just not possible."

"You'll have to do what you told me to do all those years ago: ditch the law."

"I'd love to. And what's so galling is that I haven't seen anything of the tennis because I've been so maniacally busy the last couple of weeks. We're doing an arbitration about roads being built in Iceland and I've been over there for about 12 days from dawn to dusk ploughing through documents and taking witness statements. I only got back late last night and had to catch up with a billion things this morning."

"Doesn't sound good. All this work can't be beneficial to finding the girl of your dreams."

"Tell me about it. But you've been here at Wimbledon watching all the games for nearly two weeks. Haven't you been able to find some Russian multi-millionairess who's desperate to marry an eligible Englishman?

"But how could you ever tear yourself away from your job?"

"Um, well, that's a good point, but I think I could manage it. I don't mind being a kit carrier for some blonde goddess as she and I traipse around the world together."

"OK Marcus, I'll talk to them all. See which one is the most interested."

"That's much appreciated. So anyway, tell me about the tennis. Is Javea Jackson all set to win it again?"

Terry regarded his friend with deep horror. "Are you being funny?"

"No," frowned Marcus, "I told you I've not been following it. Don't tell me he got knocked out early to some unknown."

"Are you for real?"

"Terry, what's so serious all of a sudden? Come on, tell me, I haven't even seen a paper or TV for about 12 days."

"The guy has been murdered," replied the writer through clenched teeth, whilst looking around, as it would be so stupid to be overheard saying something that 99.9 per cent of the country knew so well. "And, very recently, a girl thought to be having an affair with him was also killed. But no-one's actually certain if she was actually having a relationship with him."

Marcus became rigid and silent, and looked down at his feet. Then he relaxed his taut shoulders and, with a grimace, studied Terry's face. "That's absolutely appalling. I honestly knew nothing about it. But mate, that is particularly worrying because a guy looking like Javea Jackson came to our office late on the night before I flew to Iceland."

"Right," laughed Terry. "Why would the world's greatest tennis player personally turn up unaccompanied at a City of London law firm, way after business hours, just before he began his Wimbledon campaign? It makes no sense."

"I didn't recognise him at first," explained Marcus. "In fact, even now, I can't be totally sure it was him. He wore a long, overly large trench coat and trainers. His hair was unkempt and he was unshaven."

"Did anyone else see him?"

"No, the office was closed. Everyone had gone home, all the lawyers, secretaries, reception - even the cleaners. In fact, the main doors were security locked and I only saw him because he was hovering in the entrance just as I was crossing our reception area to get a diet coke from the vending machine."

"This is unbelievable," stated Terry. "What did he want from you?"

"Well, now it all seems really freaky, in light of what you said. But he had a battered brown A4 envelope with him and he told me he was looking for a law firm to hold some precious documents in our vaults for safekeeping. People do that from time to time, you know. They entrust lawyers with manuscripts, original certificates and so on."

"What did you do?"

"You never turn away clients; you never know who they are connected to. So I got the proforma papers that we get people to sign in these circumstances and I told him that our storage fee was £250 per annum. He filled the forms in very speedily and signed hurriedly and gave me cash; crisp 50s. Then he shook hands, took my business card and was gone."

"So his signature said Javea Jackson?"

"Actually, no. The form and his signature both stated he was called Banjul West. The whole thing was a bit surreal, actually. He told me to read his documents as soon as I had time because he said they were 'enlightening'. I didn't have a clue what he was on about, but our clients pay an annual fee for storage and the form they sign includes wording saying that we will review the documents we are holding once we've had them for 12 months, just as a formality before we send out an invoice for the cost of another year's storage. At the end of the day I'm bound by Law Society rules and his papers are protected by client confidentiality provisions. Like you know, if I violated them, I might as well be dead."

"But don't you see - I have to read all that," insisted Terry. In haste, he told Marcus about the police enquiry and his love for WPC Sassi. He didn't like Marcus' reply, which seemed to centre on the fact that nothing could happen without the police getting a court order.

"You have to understand. I must see the documents," persisted Terry.

Marcus saw, a little late, the wild streak in Terry's eyes and relented unwillingly. "OK, OK, but not tonight. It'll soon be getting on for midnight and there's no way I'm going back to the City. And anyway, there's one other thing."

"What?"

"I think I lost my office keys on the train. They must have fallen out of my pocket. As soon as I can get hold of my secretary tomorrow, I'll let you know immediately."

Chapter 29

Terry winced with displeasure as he sat in Wimbledon Village's Cafe Rouge on Saturday morning. One of the more hysterical British newspapers carried the headline "GUILTY!" and underneath was a picture of Holly with her racket in front of her face. An enterprising photographer had obviously taken the snap, knowing full well that the image portrayed a criminal behind bars.

The story was based on the fact that the paper had come to know that Holly's parents, father Don and mother Trey, had already flown out of England the day before, and were now back in Florida. The thrust of the piece was that there had obviously been a terrible argument between the daughter on the one hand, and the parents on the other, due to the latter's strong belief that they were shielding a double murderer. A few anonymous neighbours of Don and Trey were quoted, with all the comments being along the lines of "you would never have considered Holly could be a killer, but now just look at the situation she's in". The final sentence of the journalistic hyperbole said provocatively: "Miss Fleming was again unavailable for comment last night - but if she thinks we're wrong in our facts, she's free to sue us."

BBC's tennis coverage, in their pre-final analysis, chose to rely on footage from Angela's news conference following her semi-final downing of Jacalyn Jeanice. The regal star sported a black T-shirt with the golden word "VIP", and she fingered the gold and diamond necklace around her neck which declared her name in striking italics, whilst saying coolly: "Naturally I think

I'm ready to take my first Wimbledon. I wouldn't make my way to the final just to lose. Holly's a good player, for sure, but I believe the crowd will be on my side and I think they like what I'm all about. Y'know, I like to entertain and it amuses me how much the English like to write about me in papers and magazines. Your photo guys seem to be mad about me for some reason. And I can't move an inch without signing so many autographs, but to be appreciated, that's the biggest compliment."

Terry, who had been present when those words had been uttered, couldn't help but think that wily Angela was overstating her popularity in a naked bid to enhance her fan base. However, he knew that there were many who were obsessed by Angela's looks, and it was true that the press was always keen during Wimbledon to use glamour to sell more newspapers. More importantly, he hoped dearly that umpire Jon Smartson would prove to be an impartial arbiter in the afternoon, and would show no favouritism to his sometime mistress.

On the plus side, Terry - though somewhat put out by Marcus' refusal the previous evening to obtain the Javea papers without hesitation - took the view that there must be something there that would shed light on the murders. But, then again, maybe not. There was no reason for Javea to be called Banjul West and Marcus was not the most astute person about non-legal matters. By the guy's own admission, he couldn't be certain he had been dealing with Javea himself. Suddenly, Terry recalled that Marcus didn't have the best eyesight, either - that was another reason to doubt the whole story.

The reporter checked his mobile for the umpteenth time so far that day; but, irritatingly, Marcus was yet to make contact. It crossed Terry's mind that perhaps Marcus had already checked the papers in the office and realised that they had absolutely nothing whatsoever to do with Javea Jackson. Maybe the lawyer was now being craven and felt too cowardly to admit that truth.

Aside from Terry, both finalists were also deep in thought. Holly had decided, after a fitful sleep all alone in her rented mansion, that she would win the title for Terry Proudley and dedicate the victory to him. She had already been briefed that the police would probably arrest her on the suspicion of two murders as soon as the prize ceremony completed. They would not even allow her to give an interview for TV on court before hauling her away for intensive questioning.

Angela was excessively nervous, despite the imperturbable exterior she had conjured up in the press conference. Terry had ruined her day when he turned up in Cannes, and now Karan had been arrested, and as for Smartson ... he wasn't speaking to her and she was clueless as to how he'd call any close balls in the final. Would they be adjudged in her favour or Holly's? The only blessing was that her boyfriend was tied up on some mega-business deal and may not reach London in time; given all the problems with which she was mixed up, she reckoned that the absence of one more complicating factor was a very good thing.

Elsewhere, in central London, in a side road just off the Strand, Marcus Jones was walking in agitated manner towards the law office where he worked. He had retrieved office keys from his disgruntled secretary a little earlier at Liverpool Street station, and he currently felt exasperated with Terry. What was so urgent about today? Why couldn't the man wait until Monday morning to see these papers? It was so unjust. Terry got to see tennis nearly every day of the year and now it looked like Terry would deprive him, Marcus, of even seeing the Wimbledon final on television! The thought particularly aggravated him since he had something of a liking for the delectable form of Angela de Jong.

As the drab grey building came into view, Marcus experienced the familiar uncomfortable stab of pain and pathos in the pit of his stomach. His life was full of stress, backache and dissatisfaction - and he never understood now why he had urged Terry to break free from the law, whilst consigning himself to such an unhealthy and dejecting occupation. With a melancholic spirit, he unlocked the entrance doors at their top and bottom and moved moodily into the dispiriting reception area. The couches for visiting clients were grey and dismal, and the booklets left out for them to read were all about double taxation treaties and European Competition Law. Marcus let the blues engulf him. He ached for excitement and to be extricated from his conventional predicament. It was madness to be doing favours for friends when you could be staring at Angela de Jong for the next two hours, even if that pleasure would have been possible only thanks to the small screen.

Chapter 30

Angela de Jong wore a sleeveless white top with pale blue piping, together with minuscule white shorts. Her silky brown tresses were scraped back into a beguiling bunch. The ballboy throwing balls to her at the start of the warm-up gazed favourably at her long eyelashes and confident countenance.

Holly bounced on her feet as she traded ground strokes with Angela. The No 1 seed from Florida looked defenceless and weak, but the courtside lensmen were more interested in capturing her thigh when the slit in her skirt afforded the opportunity. Holly mentally blocked out the cameras' whirring and looked up at the audience. She felt her legs go to jelly when she realised that none of the faces looked sympathetic to her cause. Terry, viewing from the press enclosure, thought she looked lost and even tinier than usual.

Jon Smartson, in the umpire's chair, called: "One minute," and the girls began practising their serves. There was an expectant buzz of conversation in the stadium and Holly felt the sickness in her stomach as she stretched to whack a serve.

Around the world, over a billion people were glued to their televisions, watching every movement and every facial expression of the two finalists. Terry himself felt his own imbalance, and feared that Holly was about to play her last ever professional tennis match.

It was a bad omen when Holly opened the final with a tentative double fault. As she did so, Marcus Jones was locating the folder of Banjul West in his firm's vast array of archived files. He relaxed slightly when he saw the battered A4 envelope and he chose to lock up the strong room before reviewing the papers in the relative comfort of his office.

It worried him to have to now see what Banjul West had deposited at Devizes Tenterden. As so often with the law, he found it reassuring to put off something potentially unpleasant by first resorting to diversionary tactics. He went to the reception area and fed the money into the vending machine to obtain a restorative diet coke. Then he made for the pantry area and fixed himself a large mug of very bitter black coffee.

A few minutes later, fortified by the combined potent liquids, he returned to his seat and breathed deeply before starting to read Banjul West's documentation. The first page was so explicitly worded that Marcus believed a lawyer may have been behind its drafting:

> "To whoever reads this first, I should point out that my real name is not Mr Banjul West; it is, in fact, Mr Javea Jackson and I am a professional tennis player and the current Wimbledon Champion. If, for any reason, it should become known to the holder of these papers that I have died or been incapacitated, I do hereby irrevocably state that the entirety of this bundle must be handed immediately, and on a strictly confidential basis, to Mr Terry Proudley, tennis correspondent of London's Evening Echo."

Marcus didn't read beyond that. He immediately 'phoned Terry's mobile, but it was switched off. He left a text message imploring the writer to come urgently to central London. He considered hotfooting it himself to Wimbledon, but realised that without a ticket, he would never gain entry.

Marcus read on, but the names Drew L Todd, Jon Smartson and Blanca Alessandra meant nothing to him. He kept looking at his own mobile, willing it to ring, but actually Terry had inadvertently left his 'phone in the press centre, and the match was continuing.

Angela and Holly were holding their serves with alacrity, and had reached 3-3 in the first set. When Holly stood to start her next service game, she felt a sudden gust of wind and as her skirt flew up, she heard the inevitable noise of many cameras recording the moment. She glanced down the court towards Angela, crouching in the receiver's position with her racket ready for action. The next thing Holly knew was that the sun had given way to cloud and the changing light caused her to serve a fault into the net. Undeterred, she bent her knees well and delivered a high-kicking top spun second serve, which Angela had no option but to meet on her backhand above shoulder height. The return was mid-court and inviting; Holly duly dispatched it crosscourt for an outright winner. Soon after that, open umbrellas started to be flourished around the stands, and rain was falling quite hard by the time Holly made it 4-3. The referee suspended play and the ground staff had covered the grass before either player had vanished from public view.

Terry felt for his pocket to check for his 'phone, and flew into a panic when he came to know it wasn't on his person. He scrambled to the press centre where he saw Marcus' message and his colleagues overheard him yelling via his mobile to the lawyer: "I'm on my way; I'll come straight to Devizes Tenterden." From there he ran out of Wimbledon and hailed a passing black taxi by the main gates and already he was only concerned about Javea's unorthodox bequest.

But it was a bad situation for Terry. The cabbie was a stereotypically bluff Londoner with a checked cloth cap and rasping voice. Once he had extracted from Terry that he was a tennis journalist, there was an instant desire to engage his captive passenger in a spirited dialogue.

"Do you reckon these ladies are worth the same money as the gents, mate? What's your verdict?"

"I think they deserve the equal pay, yes," replied Terry, a little guarded. "If the game is measured on entertainment value, they merited parity, in my opinion."

"No, guv'nor, you've got it all wrong. The gents play five sets, them girls only three. So no way should they get the same."

"That's one way of looking at it," responded Terry, determined to hide his rising exasperation, which was compounded by the squeaking windscreen wipers of the taxi, which were losing a combat against ferocious rain. "But the women players probably have much longer rallies than the men. The ball is in play for longer and that's what tennis is all about. It was never meant to be a serve-dominated contest."

"I disagree, mate, I disagree. The matches are shorter so pay them less, I say."

"But what makes people watch tennis?"

"What do you mean?"

"Well, the reason people watch a sport is because they feel an affiliation with one of the protagonists. And that means the players have to have character and personality. People can only get involved and emotional about a game of any sport if they feel some bond with the people playing that game. It's been the case for some time now that the women players are striking more of a chord with the general public. They are interesting to armchair fans in a way that most of the men haven't been for a long time. Take the tabloids. They are interested in the personal lives of the female stars, but on the men's side, only Javea Jackson meant as much to them. The fact is that women pro players are making that transition into fashion, music, films, design. I strongly believe that if you are bringing people in through the gate, if you are a box office attraction, then you deserve the plaudits and money that goes with it."

"But the girls can't hit it hard like that guy Javea used to. He was different class. He was in the back of this very cab once. Such a great fella, and when…"

"You'd be surprised," countered Terry. "If you were on a tennis court trying to play Natalie Sloane or Holly Fleming, you'd be amazed at the pace of the ball and their athleticism and speed."

"Don't talk to me about Holly Fleming," retorted the cabbie. "She's a murderer, isn't she, when all's said and done."

Chapter 31

As the taxi neared Devizes Tenterden, Terry saw fidgety Marcus waiting by the kerbside. Having paid off the garrulous cabbie, the reporter turned to his friend and asked: "So, what have you got for me?"

"I'm so glad you're here," said Marcus, as he led the way into the characterless building. "It'll all make much more sense to you, but what I seem to have is Javea Jackson's memoirs in unpublished, working draft format."

They took the lift to the first floor and walked to Marcus' own office. "I took copies of all his papers," explained the lawyer, "so that you and I can go through them together. You never know, you might welcome my legalistic advice."

"Let's see what he's saying first," cautioned Terry, "although if there's anything relevant to the murder enquiry, I hope you won't mind if I inform WPC Sassi."

"I think that should be fine," said Marcus in a slightly vague voice. "I suppose, strictly in law, I would be obstructing the course of justice if I was fixed with constructive knowledge and did not disclose it."

"Whatever," remarked Terry as he sat down at the visitor's chair opposite Marcus' own. In between them stood the advocate's expansive oak table, cluttered with memoranda, reference books, notes and files.

"Well, here it is!" exclaimed Marcus, handing over original hand-written papers. "I'll make do with a photocopy. Oh, by the way, I just checked the Internet. There's still a rain break with Holly leading 4-3 in the first set."

Terry didn't respond. Instead, heedless to the person in his presence, he sank into deep concentration and began reading the top page which Javea had written in scratchy, inconsistent black pen scrawl:

"Gambia

Whenever I'm travelling around the world and want to be incognito, I do the things all celebrities do, like wear sunglasses, baseball caps and hoods. And I also try to check in to hotels under false names, to try to kid myself that I won't be disturbed and that I can still be anonymous and free.

My favourite pseudonym is Banjul West, but most readers of this book will have no idea why that is. And I guess I'll have to think up another alias now I've told you about this one!

Very few of you will have visited West Africa, and even less of you will have visited the Gambia. Why should you have been there? After all, it's only a tiny country which is basically a sub-set of Senegal. The population is about 1.4 million and because of extreme poverty, the life expectancy is only about 50 years. Buy any guidebook and the facts will hit you immediately: about 200 out of every 1,000 children die before they're five. Illiteracy is high, unemployment is high - and no-one can really afford proper food.

Anyway, the capital of this country is Banjul, a coastal city which gives way to the Atlantic Ocean. It's a decaying place, but full of humanity and the bright African sun is far more vivid than any in Europe. The market is full of all types of commodities and is a riot of human activity. It reawakens your senses! All the sports gear is counterfeit - at least, it was when I was there - and involves outrageous (or courageous?) misspellings of names like adidas and Reebok. When I pointed that out to one tradesman, he said in all seriousness that there had been some recent printing errors at the factories of these companies!

No doubt you'll ask why I went to Banjul. The answer is simple. I was 16 years old and already felt like I was an adult who had been given too much luck for one lifetime. I considered who I was as I wanted to be a better person. So I thought about what talents I had. Obviously I was really just a tennis player. So I contacted the International Tennis Federation and told them I was determined to do something in an underprivileged country because maybe in 50 years' time there'll be many Africans in the men's top 100. I offered to play an exhibition match and they recommended the Gambia. When I got to Banjul - only a six-hour flight from London - I was overwhelmed by the massive heat and the marching band which played raucous music to welcome me.

They drove me through shanty towns interspersed with beautiful landscapes to the Atlantic Hotel in Banjul. It was set back from the uneven road and local boys glared aggressively as we went through the main gates. They obviously had no jobs and no prospects - no wonder they hated me. But I was oblivious at that time and was heartened when the staff brought me a local juice drink and then showed me to a well-maintained, clean room two floors up. I went on to the balcony and fell in love with the hotel's pool area below and the beach beyond, leading to the ocean. I could see girls with trays of fruit on their head waiting behind the hotel's walls, hoping they could sell some sweet mangoes to the tourists traversing the sands en route to a swim.

The idea was that I would play Gambia's male No 1 player on the lone court at the Atlantic Hotel. The surface was bumpy and the court seemed oppressive. On all sides there was dense undergrowth and bushes. I could hear the birds singing boisterously amongst the foliage. I was also scared by the humidity; the court was right by the sea. But the biggest obstacle was that hardly anyone would see us play and so my muscular opponent, who they simply called Sampras (because they knew no other tennis names), sorted it out so that, instead, we competed on a makeshift grass court in the bumpy park at Banjul's July 22 square. The whole thing was nearly ridiculous as the lines were barely chalked out and the balls kept bouncing off the irregular ground at perverse angles. But I wasn't about to complain. Thousands turned up to watch and clapped with vigour and they sang songs unknown to me as we changed ends. I won without looking good, but far more importantly I touched lives and transmitted happiness via my racket. It was one of my most feel-good days.

But after that I planned to be stupid. I had a week in Gambia so I would do what all the tourists do; just lounge about the pool at the Atlantic and I'll admit I wanted to try to catch the eye of the air hostesses who were there for the week, reading their Marian Keyes' novels. But I knew they would ignore me and that I would be happy myself just reading trashy airport novels. At night I expected to ignore the disco in the Bendula Bar and lie awake in bed, covered in anti-malarial stuff, petrified that the mosquitoes would devour me. Nonetheless I felt calm inside, because the Gambia was different to the places I'd been, and I always feel more happy when I'm in a new environment that keeps me from getting bored. But then the inevitable happened - I fell in love, and fell in love badly."

"Interesting," muttered Marcus, reclining in his chair. "I wonder who he fell in love with." He moved the computer mouse on his desk and made a couple of clicks. "Looks like they're back on court, Terry. It's four all now."

"Aha, thanks. Let's read on, see who stole his heart."

They reverted to the papers and were soon back in the world of Javea Jackson:

"Before I tell you about the woman who was everything to me, I want to talk more about the Gambia.

The privileged, it seems, and that includes me, forget about the misery and helplessness which engulfs so many of our fellow human beings. Listen to the World Health Organization ('WHO'). The Gambia has been rated the 161st poorest out of 174 countries. School attendance is below 50 per cent, and even lower amongst girls. The illiteracy rate is 74 per cent, and 85 per cent among women. And the leading cause of death in this unlucky part of the planet is malaria, though thankfully addressing this appears to be high up on the Government's agenda. You'll also be heartened to know that WHO is assisting in this regard and has a multi-million dollar budget in the country. Their mission is uncomplicated: to support the populace to attain the highest level of health possible.

The other part you should know is that the economy of Gambia is dependent on groudnuts, but world prices have dropped by 40 per cent. Then there's coastal erosion, which is the consequence of too much sand being involved in construction work. Some beaches have almost sunk without trace!

I found this all out on the day I played that exhibition match in Banjul. I had bloodied both knees very badly during the game, going for infantile dive volleys to try to excite the fans. Someone said I should take a tetanus injection, or something like that, and I was ushered to the Royal Victoria Hospital on July 22 Drive.

And then my life took its gigantic turn. There was a nurse there, a Gambian, and I'll admit it was love at first sight. She looked so impressive, smiling amongst all the mayhem, and she was quite tall and slim. I won't tell you her name, because I want to protect both her and her family from any media intrusion. I still love her to the extent that I could never get back at her in any way. So let's say her name is Lisa. It's not true, but you can know her as Lisa. I'll keep her identity private to, and beyond, my grave.

Lisa soon tended my self-inflicted wounds and then she told me that the hospital was particularly busy that day owing to its being a 'temporary Mosquito Net Insecticide Treatment Unit'. She looked into my eyes and asked: 'Don't you know about our country's bed-net dipping campaign?'

I wanted to laugh but her young face was so earnest, so serious. Suddenly tennis seemed irrelevant. It transpired that Lisa was overseeing the use of plastic buckets, a wash basin and insecticide to impregnate nets. 'It's one of the best methods to combat malaria,' she explained to me patiently. 'Here in Gambia malaria is the cause of 25 per cent of deaths in children under five. And did you realise that one child dies every 30 seconds in Africa, due to malaria?

'The tragedy is that many of my compatriots think malaria is spread by a small animal that lives in the forest. But we are trying to show that malaria can be prevented if families sleep under mosquito nets which have been treated with insecticide.'

I was bowled over by Lisa's humility and sincerity - and I spent the rest of the day at the hospital helping as best I could. For example, I was part of a group that carried nets into the sunlight so that, once insecticide-impregnated, they could dry. And I felt enriched to be there, literally playing a part in saving lives.

So I summoned up the courage to invite Lisa out that night. I didn't think she'd be able to say yes, but for some reason she did, and in the torrid darkness a hotel car took us to what I had been told was the best Indian restaurant in West Africa. It was fun being driven through streets with no lights towards the place which was called the Clay Oven in the Bakau district. OK, the name was unimaginative, but the food was excellent and we were serenaded by a Gambian man playing heartbreakingly evocative melodies on an instrument known as a 21 stringed kora.

I don't want to tell you about the private details of our relationship because that's not what I should have to do, even as an international sportsman. So respect me on that aspect. The two of us were actually very covert about all aspects of our relationship and I was much lower profile then; I hadn't achieved what I've achieved now. So the press weren't interested in what I was doing and to make doubly sure of our anonymity I stopped socialising with anyone but Lisa, and did anything else I thought was necessary to keep us secret. No-one cared much about me back then; I was just another cocky and aloof kid as far as they were concerned. All in all, I think it's fair to say that the media and those who follow tennis never found out that Lisa and I were an item. So forgive me if my account of our liaison is somewhat circumspect.

But I'm happy to share with you all the trips which Lisa and I undertook that week. She taught me to bargain in the Albert Market and one day we took the early ferry from Banjul to Barra, sighting dolphins leaping in the water. I seem to remember that some men helped us take a short boat trip to Ginak Island, which had marshes and mangrove swamps. It's funny how difficult it is to retain a memory of the best time of your life...

But I do have an abiding reminiscence of Lisa and I walking right out of the Atlantic Hotel and making our way to Banjul's premier landmark, Arch 22. Situated on Independence Drive, it was built 35 metres into the sky to celebrate a military coup in 1994. We took the steps up to the wide balcony and looked down at the city beneath us. She was an arresting sight, Lisa, and the spartan balcony area didn't bother me at all because she had totally captivated me. I would have done anything for her. I was so thrilled to be sharing Gambia's tallest building with her.

She also introduced me to her friends who happened to be the fruit sellers standing quietly outside the walls at the back of the hotel. In turn, I introduced them all to tennis and Lisa took me to meet her family who were delighted that we got along so well. They taught me about Gambia's traditional foods such as tio grio (peanut soup) and joloff rice. It made me feel good to be a part of their tight-knit group. By the time I had to go, we had made many plans and I was certain that we would soon marry, despite all our differences. We both wanted to wed, and just the thought of it banished all my earlier doubts about living. The thing that struck me most was my newfound sense of personal well-being and the sheer pride I felt being with this girl. She was a force for good in my life, and I didn't want to let go. And there was no reason to believe that she was anything other than buoyant to have met me. I could see no troubles on our mutual horizon because it was actually Lisa who was so adamant that we should become a lifelong couple."

Terry could hear what seemed to him the distant voice of Marcus saying that Angela had taken the first set 6-4. But the newsman made no remark on the progress of the final. He was too engrossed in the literature before him, which continued:

"Our relationship was vital to me. It was as if I had lived all my life up to that time behind dark, impenetrable clouds and Lisa embodied the rays of sunshine which filtered through at first, before dominating my skies until all I could see was joyous blue above me.

I think she felt the same way about me. Of course, our time together always took place on some elevated level because I was already playing tons of tournaments and she was still working as a nurse in Banjul. But I made the trip to West Africa as often as I could. Lisa was intoxicating and I would be in a state of total joy throughout the entirety of each plane journey to see her. The pilots just couldn't get me there fast enough!

Our reunions at the airport were a picture of joint exhilaration. I took her hands in mine and we met each other's eyes and were in raptures. I believed for the first time that living made sense and I never wanted to lose our loving each other. I thought we were the luckiest pair in the whole world.

We made some fun trips, despite the ever-present tennis. I took a break after Wimbledon that year and we flew to Dubai and then on to Salalah, in the southern tip of Oman, not that far from the Yemen border. We were both deeply moved as soon as the breeze hit us from leaving the aircraft. As you touch down on the tarmac you see the small dark blue trimmed airport building in front of you, set amongst some conifer trees with an equally minor aircraft tower peeping out from the top. We looked all around and saw green landscape interspersed with sands and dark silhouettes of the mountains encircling us. It was the time of the annual khareef season, so the whole place was shrouded in low lying clouds and the mountains were so atmospheric. It looked like it was going to rain non-stop and the damp air and rampant grassy vista only made us all the more lovey-dovey.

We went on long scenic drives from our base at the Salalah Hilton and saw Job's tomb on an isolated hilltop overlooking the whole city. Only, we couldn't see anything because the mist was more like a dense fog when we visited, and visibility from the car I drove was down to less than a metre. We kept missing the correct road turning, but we were young and in love, and that made us laugh in unison. I kept on having to stop anyway because there are millions of camels there, and Lisa kept on winding down the window to inspect these proud, strong animals from close quarters. Later, back in the plush Hilton, with a standard room which was the size of a golf course, Lisa told me to make sure I married her quickly. I could hear the rolling waves from the sea just yards from where we spoke. At the time I felt a leap of fright, but I promised her that six months from then we would definitely be husband and wife.

It's true I had an initial stab of uncertainty about making a life-long commitment. But that soon went. I woke up every day thereafter in a deliriously cheerful way because it was a chance to remind myself that Lisa and I were for real. I imagined the treasure of having a child with her. Being parents would give me added security that she would never leave me and, in addition, it would be a visual symbol of our undying attachment. My tennis certainly improved. I also trained harder. I wanted to prove myself to Lisa and it helped to be ever more successful and ever fitter. I knew she was impressed by my victories and my always improving body shape.

Lisa also accompanied me a few weeks later to the US Open in New York. What a tournament! My memories of that heady time are all jumbled up. We jogged happily together early each morning in Central Park and, if I had a day off from a match, we lazed late afternoon in the park's lush and pleasurable Sheep's Meadow. Lisa was awed by the tournament site, Flushing Meadow. It didn't matter that it was sweaty and humid, with too much red brick and concrete on display. For Lisa, she was entranced by the many food outlets selling overstuffed sandwiches and the like, plus she found it clever to have a cafe with TV screens showing play on various courts. She coaxed me once or twice into sharing her ice cream over-indulgence!

We both were attracted by the change of mood each day as matches which had started in daylight ended up at their climax under bright floodlights. Lisa was fascinated by the Arthur Ashe Stadium Court and its sheer scale, and I was able to express to her the adrenaline rush it was for me playing there in front of 23,000 punters, with constant perspiration trickling down my back. One thing I adored was the rock music blaring out at the changeovers. The pop concert atmosphere drove me on and stimulated me to push myself even harder. New York was good for me and in fact I felt very safe there. The people were life-affirming. For instance, I never tired of being told in the States: 'Have a nice day', and it amused Lisa to hear chauvinistic male fans shouting: 'That was out, baby angel' whenever a female player dared to query a linecall.

I also remember that autumn I played an exhibition in Zurich and we stayed in gorgeous Lucerne, and took a lake trip that alerted me to the realisation that I had never been to such an enchanting place. It was absolutely idyllic.

Our romance continued perfectly and we never argued. It wasn't that we were being overly polite; the fact was that we just got on brilliantly and found no points of disagreement. Lisa understood that tennis was a priority, but she was keen to fit in, and when I asked her to fly that autumn to Edinburgh in Scotland, just for a few days, she was very willing to do so. We ate a large Scottish breakfast at the Caledonian hotel and walked up to Edinburgh Castle, to sense its vastness and timeless appeal. Bagpipes were playing as we looked down at Princes Street, the main shopping hub, and in front of it our eyes were drawn to gardens that came right up to the castle's edge. I looked at Lisa and she flashed a smile at me and I knew we were on the same track in life. After that we roamed the city, taking in Holyrood Park with its spectacular mountain, Arthur's Seat, and we walked along Queen's Drive to see the oddly named park attractions such as Dunsapie Loch and St Margaret's Loch. We ran some of the way and playfully tried to catch each other. I rolled down the hilly slopes and Lisa waited for me to collapse into her waiting arms. It was like something out of a film. Everything was too perfect, like the Kalpna restaurant we loved.

There was only one last completely good time with Lisa, which took place when we holidayed in the Maldives. We took a villa on Kurumba Island and forgot about everything apart from each other. Aside from taking an air taxi one day to see another of the islands, we hardly emerged from our villa - except to eat succulent Indian food at the aptly named Kurumba Mahal. To me, it was always paradise when it was only the two of us.

Soon, however, our relationship began to unravel and there was nothing I could do to stop it spinning horribly and uncontrollably away from me. It all seemed to start when I took a trip to the Gambia for my birthday. I loved Lisa's company, as always, but I sensed her family were having second thoughts about their daughter being with a rich tennis star. I think they resented our togetherness. Whatever. Perhaps it would have been all right if Lisa hadn't taken me out on a trip just hours before I had to catch a flight from Banjul to connect with another flight which would take me to my next tournament. As the minutes ticked away and it looked like I would miss the Banjul plane, I lashed out verbally, spilling my tension before her, and though I never criticised her directly for the mishap, and we ostensibly forgot about it, I now look back with the view that that unfortunate incident was the beginning of our end. It was the first occasion I had raised my voice and I must have appeared absurdly uptight and selfish. I was really upset that I had lost any semblance of cool in front of her. Sadly, it happened less than six months after she had asked me to marry her, and the rest of our tale is now a history, a very painful and personal history, which I cannot get away from."

Terry looked up. "I'm just going out," said Marcus, who was already at his office door. "I fancy some cigarettes and I'll try to get us something to eat. There's not much round here though; the City's pretty much dead on the weekend."

The journalist made a non-committal sound and returned to Javea's draft autobiography. It didn't feel good, intruding on a dead man's private sorrow, but someone had to find out the truth. And the truth was obvious. There was no murderer; Javea had clearly never recovered from being dumped by the girl he called Lisa. It was apparent that Javea had fought to overcome his melancholia, and had done superbly well to lift a Wimbledon crown. Yet his struggle had been in vain, and it was he himself who used poison to commit suicide, perhaps aided and abetted by a person or persons unknown, who should have known better. But that still didn't explain why Larissa had been killed. Only Holly could have done that. Or could it actually have been someone else? For the first time, Terry thought the conundrum through more analytically and logically. Javea had been in great demand from assorted women. Angela could have plotted to catch him with her charms, perhaps as a way to stop Javea from disclosing anything negative about her. Jacalyn was crazy about him. Perhaps Natalie was, too. There were probably others who were also drawn to the handsome 18 year-old star. Any of those girls may have been angered by Larissa beating them to the bounty. There was, as a result, a reason for other women - not just Holly - to want to murder LaDame. It was conceivable that any girl who had hankered after Javea may have yearned to cancel out the last girl who was with him, namely Larissa. It was also possible, reflected Terry, that someone might have killed Larissa if that person believed that it was Larissa who had either eliminated Javea, or had incited him to eliminate himself.

The writer had a strong recollection that Larissa, by her own admission, had not loved Javea, but was well aware that her memoirs about life with the tennis champ were worth far more if he were dead. If Larissa or her associates had somehow encouraged Javea to commit suicide - or killed him themselves - then anyone who had an overflowing passion for Javea could easily have been provoked into doing away with Larissa.

Terry turned the page, and perused the next section, under a chapter heading entitled "Darkness":

"Nothing destroyed me as much as the end with Lisa. I didn't have much self-confidence before I met her, and I had less than none by the time we parted. In my naivety I had assumed that she thought me too good to lose. But by the end I saw her pleasure in spending time socialising amongst men of her own national-ity, and I found it hard to take. I would travel from all over the world just to find a few days with her, but she seemed off-hand and more and more she made no effort to speak English - when in my presence - to her family and friends. Before, everyone spoke English when I was there, but that courtesy disappeared. I felt alienated and rejected, and when I broached the subject, she would insist nothing had changed, although I knew it had.

I don't want to talk too much about the death throes of the relationship, but I will admit that I am far from over the mental carnage it wreaked upon me. Our time together only lasted 11 months, but it will never leave my ever-waking moment. I have had two girlfriends since then, but it's hard to recapture the magic when your brain is always heading backwards. Those two women, with the greatest respect to them, had no chance at all, despite being nothing but giving to me. And in actual fact, one of them is still my girlfriend as I write this, but she won't be by the time you read this. Don't get me wrong, I never want to make anyone unhappy. And the knowledge that I am days away from breaking off with my fiancée breaks my heart. Yes, I am having suicidal thoughts. I also know that, even if I get through this slump, what I've just written is probably too raw to see the light of day. But in case one day I give up the fight and call time on my existence here on earth, I want it to be known that I never meant to inflict harm upon Holly Fleming.

But another lady has, indirectly, tortured me for longer than I care to remember. She and her family need to get help because I feel they might just hound me to death. If anything gives you an insight into the dark side of fame, the clichéd price we pay, then my experience in Rome and beyond will be all the evidence you need. I went to Italy about a week after the final separation from Lisa. I was in a very bad state and could see nothing to live for. The funny part is that things can always get worse than the present. I didn't appreciate that then. But I do now. I wasn't looking for another girlfriend. In my mind, Lisa remained an irreplaceable goddess. I should have understood that my heart would be hungry for a way to come to terms with the break-up. At the time I was feeling my way mechanically through each minute of each day; I believed that nothing good would ever happen again.

All the players that week were staying at the inevitable five star, which was perched on a hill overlooking Rome and in particular overlooking the Foro Italico tennis club, where the clay courts are set amongst white marble statues and glorious high trees. Everyone else was basking in the aesthetic beauty of it all, but I remained steadfastly in the doldrums. Apart from practice and matches, I stayed in my room and wondered about the injustice of losing Lisa. Then there was a knock on the door and the chambermaid came in. I could see at once that she was my age and she talked in fast and furious Italian. I mumbled my apologies so she switched to halting English. Like a fool I responded immediately to her smile and youthful enthusiasm to clean the room properly. She had wavy shoulder length hair and was perhaps a bit skinny. I didn't mind.

We talked about the tennis, her studies in art, the economy in Italy. Her name was Maria and, Maria, I now wish I had never met you. If only you had obtained a temporary job in another hotel, or on a different floor to mine. If I had never met you, I think I might have recovered from the Lisa debacle. But instead you came into my life and you seriously believed you had a future with me.

The next day I was on court and at that time I was little known there. The crowds were sparse. I looked over to my left as I stood at the end of one game, waiting to receive serve in the next, and I heard a girl cry out: 'Good luck, Javea, good luck!' Then I saw Maria waving at me and grinning broadly and with an easy-going chirpiness. I felt so bad that I was feeling so sad when she wanted me to feel so good. So I took care to win the match and thanked her as she waited at the side of the court when I was on my way to the locker room. I glimpsed the respect and appeal in her eyes and it shocked me to know that I could still be at all desirable when my whole body language screamed defeat.

Over the next few days she took me to the must-see bits of her city. We held hands and threw coins over our backs into the Trevi Fountain. From the top of the Spanish Steps we took in the view of the tourists below and the great flower displays. We kissed in Villa Borghese - a place we seemed to have all to ourselves - and took a 15 minute hot air balloon ride which accentuated our mutual attraction.

I made her try on daring dresses, skirts and T-shirts in boutiques like the one called Roman's. Yes, it was great to treat her and we had a ball in the jeans shop, Energie, where she helped me to pick out a whole new trendy wardrobe for myself. I defy anyone not to feel a little revived by Rome. The weather's good, the ice cream is even better, and the people are stylish and take a pride in their appearance, without being offensive or threatening to foreigners. I only wish I could play a tennis match inside the perfectly circular Coliseum, built in 72 AD!

Maria and I had a lunch one day in the shadows of the Pantheon in Piazza della Rotonda. We were at an outside table and we tucked into the best, most fresh and tasty pizza which money could buy. The Pantheon's about the same age as the Coliseum and it hypnotises you with its temple-like structure. In fact, Maria told me it was originally a temple and then was converted much later into a Christian church. She said the Pantheon's dome was the first dome ever built in the world. It felt spiritual for us to stand right beneath the dome inside the Pantheon. It's the only source of light the building has, and as we cuddled in that unpretentious shaft of sunshine, Maria whispered to me: 'We are now both connected, as a twosome, with the heavens - where you and I shall one day sit together.' I put that statement down to Italian charm because I didn't have any real overwhelming spark of sensuality for Maria. I was just trying to scrape through each day without wanting to cry.

Despite all the good aspects of Rome, I don't see why I had to get entangled in trouble. But that was a long way off when I was with Maria, my 'girlfriend' of two or three days' standing, and she was showing off great stuff like the Fontana di Tritone to me, which is an excellent sculpture and fountain with an old hotel as its backdrop. I liked her company, I was honoured she wanted to spend her time with me, but something told me that by the end of the week, I would fly out of Rome and never see her again. As bad as it seemed, the thought didn't perturb me. I just wanted to know that women still wanted me and I felt that I could get back at Lisa and restore a bit of my ego by proving that, because others fancied me, Lisa had been wrong to walk away.

On our last afternoon together we walked down to a chapel in an area called Cosmedin. Maria was really happy because it was called 'Santa Maria'. And just inside the chapel entrance, on the left, was an ancient stone face set in the wall, with a slightly smiling, cracked visage and a mouth large enough for you to put your hand in. I knew it from the film *Roman Holiday*, when Gregory Peck put his hand in and acted as if he was being pulled in by the mouth eating his hand and arm. It was called Bocca della Verita. Maria explained that if you were a liar, your arm got eaten by the mouth. I put my hand in and she asked me if I loved her. I said 'yes'. Nothing happened. But I knew I had lied. And that's when Maria commented casually: 'Isn't it funny, this is Santa Maria and my name's Maria and the mouth's called Bocca della Verita - the Mouth of Truth - and my half-sister's name is Verita.' I gave it no thought; it didn't seem so interesting to me. Instead, I kept harking back to Gregory Peck in that film *Roman Holiday* with Audrey Hepburn. Was it possible that in real life they had fallen a little in love in the Eternal City? That movie always haunts me. At the end of the day Peck, who plays a journalist, walks away from the press conference, knowing that his 24 hours' adventure with Audrey (a princess) will never be repeated. I hated that moment. It reminded me of the end with Lisa. When I see *Roman Holiday* I want to scream out loud that there should be a 'Roman Holiday II' when the pair meet up again and live happily ever after. Sad endings are too evocative of real life for me.

How foolish I was to lie that day to Maria; I only did it because I didn't want to hurt her feelings and I thought that my noble falsehood would simplify an otherwise tricky moment. Instead I dug myself into a hellish hole. When I didn't return Maria's calls in the weeks that followed, I suddenly started receiving messages from this stranger Verita. They were unsettling and accused me of taking advantage of Maria. I just carried on as usual, still deep in my misery, and yet I noticed that I was scared to answer my 'phone and that was no good. I changed my number and the problem died for a while. But then I started receiving letters at tournaments accusing me of ruining Maria's psychological state and that I had better watch out. I am not condoning what I did, but the relationship was consensual while it lasted, and my opinion is that Maria and Verita were hoping to capitalise on my burgeoning celebrity status. I wish they could have realised that I was unbelievably sad at that time and couldn't have been any lower. In a way, I don't think I was responsible for my actions in Rome. I was still mentally bereft and insane due to the havoc Lisa had put me through. Furthermore, people have to realise that you cannot force a relationship. Verita thinks she can perpetually browbeat me month after month and that eventually I'll fall in love with her half-sister. But that's not the way love works. My life would have been far easier if I could have fallen for Maria the way I had for Lisa - but it never happened.

I am sure when you read this you may well take the view that I should have taken better care of a star-struck chambermaid who came face to face with her hero.

But remember that Maria and I are the same age and still going through growing pains. Teenagers break up all the time - without comeback. Everything that we did together was by mutual agreement, and my only fault is that I didn't stand up and say unequivocally: 'I am not in love with you, Maria.'

Like I say, if I wasn't a tennis star, I'm sure Maria and Verita would have forgotten me by now. I just want to say via this book that these two should grow up and leave me in peace. I am not their property. And I do not take kindly to any threats or false accusations. I hope that now I have aired this topic, these two will see reason. Yes, I could involve the police, but that would only escalate the matter for all concerned. It may even make them all the more determined to harm me or those close to me. I will always be grateful for my Rome experience - but girls, enough is enough. It's time for you both to let go because, in truth, I think one way or another ... you might just kill me. I have endured the attentions of you two stalkers for too long and you've forced me now to speak out about your harrowing tactics. I've kept it secret from everyone for what seems an eternity, but not anymore."

Terry felt a stirring of emotion inside. He remembered the vibrant, crusading Javea with whom he had conversed during that late, balmy Middle Eastern night. Then there was that email from the player himself just before he was due on Wimbledon's Centre Court. Soon after that came death for Javea Jackson. And throughout this chain of plaintive occurrences, it had always been Javea's wish that Terry should discover all the leads that would direct him to the truth. But what was the reality? Had Javea really been massacred, or had he been pushed by multiple others to his own desperate conclusion by suicide?

Abruptly, the silence in Marcus' office was violated. Verita was there, leaning on the doorframe, smart and competent in her police uniform, and with a wide grin on her magnificent face. Her arms were folded casually across her chest. Terry's eyes widened involuntarily as he absorbed the sublime sight.

"Aren't you the real-life detective," cooed Verita, verbally toying with the seated Terry.

"I, er, I mean, it's great as ever to see you," replied Terry reflexively. "How come you knew I was here?"

"I was on duty inside the court today," said Verita coolly. "I scoured the press seats and it amazed me not to see the sport's most adorable journalist. So I made my enquiries in and around the press centre and hey presto! Some bright spark had obviously been eavesdropping on you, and heard you were on your way to Devizes Tenterden. It only took me a bit more research to find out that you were somehow willing to break off from the Wimbledon final to come to a law firm. And on a Saturday! When they don't even work! So I thought to myself, 'There's something brewing here. I wonder what it is?' And that's what brought me here."

"Well, it's good that you could make it."

"What are you doing here?"

"Oh, nothing much."

"So strange, though, don't you think? You being here."

"Why?"

"I mean, you being a tennis journo and all. It being Wimbledon's final day. You not liking the law very much as a profession. But suddenly you're risking your job at the Evening Echo by hotfooting it to the City for an afternoon's spot of legal research."

Terry, uncomfortable, tried to conceal the papers he was analysing - without making his manoeuvre obvious. "You see, I am not very ambitious," he offered. "Remember how I went to Jersey with you that day to help with the enquiry. I had no approval from my boss. But I was there, wasn't I. Just to help you, Verita, you remember."

"Quit the games," spat Verita, advancing to the desk. She stood where Marcus normally sat, and leant her palms on the table. "I just met your mate Marcus outside, looking hopelessly for a fag. He's going to be a long time because I reminded him that his best bet is to go to Embankment tube station for that. It was very kind of him to let me know that you were busy reading the memoirs of Javea Jackson. So they really do exist, do they?"

"Um, yes, they do. You, er, you never told me that you knew Javea. Why was that, Verita? Why did you hide that from me?"

"You've gotten too close, mate. Way too close. Why couldn't you just shut up and leave this all to us, the police. And now you're intimating that me and little Maria are mentioned in that disgusting book of his. Well, now you ask, let me give you what you press jokers always want: the truth! I killed Javea - so now you know."

Terry peered at Verita. He was still sitting down, but venomous Verita stood over him from the other side of Marcus' desk. Terry said: "Why were you after him, Verita? What had he done that was so bad?"

"Simple. My little sister was never the same after her week of whirlwind romance with Jackson. I had to nurse her like a baby. But she couldn't pull herself together again. She was so madly in love with him and he just threw her out of his life. Like rubbish! No-one treats my family like that and lives! So I kept contacting him to at least make him go and see her, to try to make a life with Maria! Cos Maria had no life! She was so young and pathetic and already she talked as if her entire life was over and meaningless! I couldn't bear it, can't you see. About two weeks after he dallied with Maria in Rome he got into another tie-up. This time it was with Holly Fleming. Oh, don't ask me how Maria came to know about it. The girl's totally immersed in tennis and corresponds with like-minded people all over the world about it! So when she found out that she had meant so little to Javea she became even more disturbed. I was frightened for her. She was about to do herself real harm. Now, maybe I could have coped with all that, but then Jackson told me when I threatened him in one 'phone call that he was going to blag about me and Maria in some book. It was the final straw. As far as I was concerned he'd destroyed Maria and now he wanted to destroy her again - and me - in some stupid autobiography! By this time I had deliberately done all the right things to become a lowly ranked police officer in London. I volunteered for duty at Wimbledon, and charmed the right guys in the force to make sure I was guarding Rectory Orchard."

"How did you know Javea was staying there?"

"Maria again. Her underground tennis network knew all that. And now, before I kill you, let me explain how I annihilated Javea Jackson."

"And Larissa LaDame?"

"I nearly forgot. You're right. Her, too."

Terry looked down for a despairing moment and, when he looked up, Verita was waving a small pistol at his head. He put his hands up and Verita smiled in a hostile, lethal manner, before carrying on. "It'll give me such happiness to explain everything ... before you're eliminated. You are pointless, you know that? A girl like me comes into your life and, bang, within a few minutes you're laughably hooked. You know nothing about me and yet that's no bar, is it. You'd fall in love with anyone who was stupid enough to fall in love with you!"

Terry said nothing. What could he say? Verita snorted derisively before adding: "It was too easy to finish Jackson off. It all went something like this. Let me see. Oh yes, first I roped in a couple of, what shall we call them, accomplices? Whatever you label them, let me tell you one thing: they are excellent at lying to police officers! They wore hoods and sunglasses and handed a box to me outside Rectory Orchard. Inside the box, as they well knew, was a jar of marmalade which I had already doctored with rat poison. It was a cold day, the first day of Wimbledon. So cold that no-one commented on the fact that I wore gloves and stamped my feet to keep warm. That helped me, of course, as I'll prove to you. Because at a certain point in the morning I knocked on

Javea Jackson's door and told him that I had been keeping a box of gifts from some of his fans. He seemed in a really good mood and obviously he liked my looks. I said I was cold having been on duty outside his house for hours and would there be time for a very quick coffee and perhaps an autograph? He obliged me. He couldn't resist a pretty face, and mine is prettier than most. But I could see he was on edge. He said he was getting ready to go over to the courts and could I bear with him while he showered and packed his tennis bag? It all went off perfectly. But then I spied a real problem: another jar of marmalade on his table! So I said - as I had already planned to do - that I'd fix him some marmalade on toast. Supercilious bum that he was, of course he agreed. I went into the kitchen, taking the marmalade that I'd seen on the table. It pays to be over prepared. I had another type of rat poison hidden on my person. I added and mixed around that rat poison to the jar that had been on the living room table. I also took the other poisoned marmalade from the box of the "fans", and used that to spread on his toast. Soon after that, having had coffee and a little chat, I made my excuses and left. I had accomplished what I wanted: the death of Jackson without leaving any of my fingerprints behind! Within a few seconds I was back on duty. No-one was the wiser."

"No-one?"

Verita wheeled away from the desk and reverted to her earlier position in the doorway.

"Oh, so you do have a brain, after all. Well, you're quite right. Someone did see me entering Javea's house and that person must have become more and more suspicious about what they saw. And finally Larissa LaDame made contact with me. She said something about having broken her heel as she went down the steep part of Church Road towards the All England Club. And she was apparently bending down trying to fix the shoe just as I was going inside to Javea. Just my unbelievable lack of luck that such a bitch saw me right there on Rectory Orchard. But then I had a bit of fortune. Larissa was such a schemer that she didn't want to report me. She was after regular money from me to buy her acquiescence. Yes, she was a blackmailer. At first I thought I'd have to go along with her. But then I told myself that I was a killer and I could kill again. Which is what I did, having agreed to hand over cash at the toilets in the club museum! And I made sure I was wearing the same white tracksuit, and cap, that Holly favoured. So that's how I did it, Terry, and now I'll kill you right…"

"Nooo!" rang out the thunderous word of Marcus, from behind Verita's back. He grabbed both her arms and aimed the gun up to the ceiling. With his left shoulder he barged WPC Sassi sideways and she fell towards the floor. Terry leapt forward and wrestled the pistol from her grasp. For good measure Marcus shed his inhibitions and stamped his right foot into the murderer's frail spine. Verita groaned as Marcus pinned her arms down to the floor. Terry choked with relief. It was suddenly all over; he and Marcus had brought the slayer to book - and it had been achieved with all thanks to Javea's book.

Chapter 32

The Wimbledon final stood at one set all, and 6-5 to Holly in the final set. For the second time, Angela would have to step up to serve to save the match.

The TV camera opposite the umpire's chair focused on the finalists seated either side of Jon Smartson. Holly's face muscles looked tight as she bounced the face of her racket on the palm of her hand; there was a ping from the strings as she did so. Her knees were covered in a Wimbledon towel and you sensed that becoming champion would do nothing to ease her torture. In contrast, Angela sat back in her chair and ordered a ballboy to bring her water. She scanned the crowd and stretched out her golden legs. She towelled her skin with care and then the camera caught her looking up at Smartson, smiling. To anyone in the know, it looked as if some type of rapprochement had just taken place.

The crowd screamed their encouragement to Angela when the girls stood up and changed ends. Holly discerned the partisan people and thought for a moment that she, too, wouldn't support the murderer of Javea Jackson. She switched her attention to the scoreboard, seeking motivation and reassurance that she stood only four points from the first prize. And then, for her, a miracle occurred. Without warning, the numbers displaying "6-5, Fleming" disappeared from view. Frantic ballboys (instructed by the club's chairman) were scrambling to cover the board with white cloth banners which conveyed, in impromptu black marker pen, the astounding, exhilarating message: "KILLER OF

JACKSON AND LADAME HAS CONFESSED; IN POLICE CUSTODY".

The court erupted into overpowering noise as each individual within the beautiful stadium took in the news flash. Holly moved to the baseline to receive serve but found that she was crying uncontrollably. Her shoulders were undulating with the enormity of the communiqué which was stolidly declaring the words which vindicated her. And then the entire audience stood and clapped her with immense vigour. Holly wiped the tears from her eyes and held her left hand up to salute the fans' change of heart.

It was Angela's turn to look tight-lipped. She glared at Holly and sent a serve down the centre line. Holly returned the ball midcourt, and Angela rifled a forehand deep into the corner. But Holly had anticipated the move and rocketed over to her left in order to send a classic double-handed backhand down the line past the flailing racket of the advancing server. The punters arose from their seats and punched the air, delighted with what was fast becoming a genuinely rousing finale.

Still standing at the net, willowy Angela let out a shriek of suffering and turned desperately to face her pensive entourage in the players' box. Holly was meanwhile already bouncing on her light feet in the advantage court, ready for conflict on the next point.

The rally that followed was classic in quality. Tall Angela slammed down a big first serve and Holly was pinned back on the baseline for the next few shots, stretching from side to side. The spectators could not contain their admiration for Holly's retrieving abilities and there were audible exclamations of approval which were met with loud shushing sounds from others who were watching. At last Angela raced to the net having played a vicious sliced crosscourt backhand. Holly again attempted a down-the-line double-handed winner, but this time Angela was there to intercept it, and she sent an angled drop volley across the face of the net to make it 15 all.

Holly strode impassively back to the baseline in the deuce

court. She nodded her tousled head in somewhat dramatic fashion, hoping to egg herself on to glory and, if all went well, a date, or even lifetime contract, with Terry Proudley. But this time the serve out wide to her forehand was too strong. The glamour girl from Florida could only parry the ball back to Angela who had a simple backhand volley to play into the wide-open court. Thirty-fifteen.

Around the globe, a vast army of TV watchers was scrutinising the women's every move and speculating on the outcome and also commenting on the shots and physical attributes of the two warriors tussling on centre stage.

Another long point developed. Holly had to bend very low repeatedly, with her left knee brushing the hallowed turf, in order to dig out double-handed backhands from balls skimming so low that they were adjacent to her shoelaces. It looked as if the heavy sliced barrage of wily Angela would come out on top, but as the Dutch destroyer again took the net position, cunning Holly hoisted an unexpected lob that bounced just inside the baseline, far over her opponent's despairing head. Thirty-all.

Terry and Marcus were by now rushing back to the All England Club by taxi. They were listening to radio commentary of the drama as Angela served a fault. "Come on, double fault," said Terry out loud. And that's exactly what happened. "Oh, how disappointing!" bellowed the commentator. "Angela de Jong has finally lost her composure and that second serve hit the net tape and dribbled back in such a writhing manner to her side of the court. It's a double fault she may just regret for the rest of her life. Because Holly Fleming, the world No 1 and the queen of women's tennis who has been cleared of any involvement whatsoever in the Wimbledon murders, stands at championship point. What on earth is going to happen now?"

All eyes surveyed the graceful Angela as she bounced the ball deliberately and slowly. Her first serve was a fault. The TV coverage switched to show Holly move in a few steps to try to attack the susceptible second serve. Angela bravely produced a high-kicking delivery but Holly took it early, sending a double-handed backhand screaming down the line. Angela saw it late, but scrambled to her right and flicked her wrist at the last minute, just as the crowd was already bursting into sound to recognise Holly as the Champion. The lass from Amsterdam had only managed to throw up a high but slow-moving forehand lob.

Holly saw the ball clearly against the London sky, and had a split-second recognition that she was about to fulfil her life-long ambition and win Wimbledon. Yet the thought may have temporarily distracted, or intimidated her. The smash was an easy put away, but Holly's body was still square to the net, when she should have moved her feet to be side on. Her racket was well prepared and in position, however, so surely she would win the point. She connected with the ball and it sailed towards the baseline, far to Angela's left. It was clear that Holly had not made a clean hit and it was too soon to say if the ball would fall out or .... it finally bounced, chalk flew up, the crowds were hailing champ Holly and Angela was running to the net to shake hands. Holly raised her arms aloft, with her racket still clasped in her right hand. She had won it with a smash!

But umpire Smartson was not announcing the victory. "The ball was out," he said hurriedly. "The linesman was incorrect; I'm overruling him. The score is deuce."

Holly thought she would shatter into a million pieces right there on Court No 2. There was no Hawk-Eye on the outside courts and this was the first singles final ever played on an outside court. Smartson's heart thumped: it had not been easy to organise the overnight vandalism of both Centre Court and Court No 1, but it had been managed, and so the turf on both courts had been severely damaged, meaning that they could not be used today. The stewards had had no option but to direct the arriving fans to Court No 2, and to seat them there on a "first come, first served" basis - with later attendees having to opt for a refund and a shattered afternoon. In the back of a black cab, Terry held his head in his hands. The spectators were booing loudly, baying for

Smartson's blood.

The only amused individual at Wimbledon was Angela de Jong. So Smartson had come good after all. She knew that now everything would be all right. She looked at her enemy, Holly, and saw someone for whom the last fortnight had suddenly become too much.

The points began to get away from the American. The fans tried to lift her, but she was a spent force. The ball had been in, but had been called out by Smartson. Holly had been fighting demons for way too long, and she mentally checked out before the final ball.

When Angela, punching the air with delight and aggression, reached match point, the fire inside Holly Fleming was burning brightly. In the next rally, she whacked a ball in ire and shaken Angela replied with another short lob. This time Holly wanted to make no mistake. But her rattled mind failed to give signals to her feet … and her smash, again hit square on to the net, finished its journey in the middle of the net. Angela sank to her knees and bent forward to kiss the grass. Angela de Jong was Wimbledon Champion: 6-4, 5-7, 8-6.

*

Chapter 33

Terry felt an overpowering sadness for Holly. As the tournament was effectively over, the security guard on what was once called the South East Gate allowed him to bring Marcus into the All England Club.

As Marcus looked around like a child in the proverbial sweet shop, the journalist was stewing over the facts as conveyed by the radio commentator. It appeared that Holly had been cheated by umpire Smartson. All the papers would be full of it the very next day. The radio analysts had also said that TV replays clearly showed that Holly's smash on her match point had touched the latter part of the baseline, meaning that her shot was good and she should have been the rightful Champion.

Terry was also trying to expunge Verita from his memory. She had massacred British tennis' finest male player since Fred Perry, and terminated another human being near the Centre Court structure itself.

In the press centre, Terry watched endless replays of Holly's smash on her match point and then watched the interviews which had taken place on court at the end of the final.

Angela's translucent top did not deflect Terry's attention from her words. "It feels great to be the Champion," she told the crowds in her perfect Dutch English. "I worked for this my whole life and I think we both played superb today. Y'know, there's a lot of emotion in a final and so much has gone on this Wimbledon. I just hope the fans appreciate that this final was for them and I want to pay credit to Holly, she's an absolute star. We both deserved to win today and I'm sure Holly will want to win it from me next year. Thank you very much everyone."

There were whistles and catcalls from the stands. Angela was asked: "How did you see that smash when you were match point down?"

"Um, y'know, we are all professionals so we all abide by the calls. The umpire called it out so that's good enough for me."

"But did you see it in or out, Angela? I'm sure that's what everyone here wants to know."

"Um, y'know, I'm not going to get into all that right now. I'm the Champion and I'm thrilled to make it here. This is a culmination of all I've ever strived for. I, er, I was running to cover the court and at times like that you can't keep a fixed eye on the line and the ball, so that's why there's an umpire. I don't think I saw it. We have to play to what he says."

"But surely it was too close for him to overrule his linesman?"

"Like I said, I'm not getting into that. I played a solid match today and I'm not going to let anything spoil this moment."

"Thank you, Angela. I'm sure you'll enjoy your celebrations tonight."

Terry manufactured a short, sardonic laugh. Then his face froze as he saw Holly, the runner-up, come forward for the TV interview.

"Holly, you've done us proud. You've been proven to be an innocent young lady and you overcame death threats as well to come within a whisker of taking the title. Absolutely remarkable."

Court No 2 again became a wall of noise; there was another standing ovation for the beaten finalist.

"Thank you," replied Holly. "I am sure you all know I gave my best. I have wanted to die the last few days but the makeshift banner message gave me, uh, let's say, sustenance, and yet it just wasn't quite my championship, ultimately."

"Was the smash in or out, do you think Holly?"

"I'm afraid that it looked to me to be good. If I never win Wimbledon, that stroke will haunt me forever. I couldn't believe the overrule. After all I've been through this tournament, it was so unmanageable that I lost out like that."

"Holly, we'll let you have a shower and a good massage. The fans are proud of you. Let's hope we see you next year."

The fans gave Holly a terrific send-off, clapping her fervently as she walked from Court No 2. They continued like that for a full ten minutes. She had lost, but everyone thought she had in fact won.

"Terry," came the voice behind the writer.

He turned and there was the creamy, smiling face of Holly Fleming herself. Her black, wavy curled hair was shining once again, and her skin glowed in appreciation of him.

Other reporters looked up in surprise to see the runner-up actually in the press centre by their work stations. Yet Holly's eyes were only for Terry.

"I am so sorry," he said.

"Please, take me away from this," Holly pleaded.

"I actually have been keeping a secret," stammered Terry.

"What is it?" frowned the star.

"I have always loved you. I, er, would never have interfered between you and Javea, and I confess I lost my way the last two weeks, but I just think you're the one for me."

"And you for me," whispered Holly, as they hugged.

"By the way," Terry suddenly commented, "You never replied to my letters. I told you I admire you greatly, and find you inspirational, but…"

"That was you?!" replied Holly, laughing. "Teach me to be a better person, Terry. A better person like you. I never even read to the end of those letters, I am so sorry. I was too wrapped up in Javea and myself."

"Forget it," responded Terry gallantly. "I have an idea. Can we do something I've always wanted to do? Can we walk up from here to Wimbledon Common, just like the lovers did at the end of that 1979 film *Players*, set at Wimbledon? It ends with them walking towards a fun fair on the common."

"That was a romantic movie," agreed Holly. "The main guy in that film used to make me quiver. And now it's up to you to sweep me off my feet."

"It will be my eternal motivation," said a very happy and floating Terry.

Chapter 34

The Evening Echo's newsboys wrote enough wordage to take over the first 11 pages of the next day's paper. All of it revolved around the arrest of WPC Sassi and there were long quotes from the heroes of the hour, Terry and his friend Marcus Jones.

The back page, however, belonged to Terry himself. The banner headline read, inevitably, "THE SMASH!" and his story was as follows:

"LEGGY ANGELA DE JONG triumphed at Wimbledon yesterday 6-4, 5-7, 8-6, but the real winner was runner-up, Holly Fleming from Florida.

The American baseliner spoke to me exclusively last night about the events that saw her hit a winning smash when she had match point, only to have the point taken away from her when umpire Jon Smartson inexplicably overruled his linesman.

Said Holly: 'It's been a roller coaster Wimbledon. I've been thought by many to be a double murderer, but thank God that's now been resolved. As for the final, TV will always show that my smash caught the baseline. No-one can rob me of the truth. They can send the footage to NASA or someone like that and I am sure the labs can enhance it a million times and then I'd like to see anyone deny that in fact I won.

'I'm taking advice from the lawyers at top London firm Devizes Tenterden. Yes, in this day and age you have to litigate when unfair things happen. Deep down I will always consider myself this year's Wimbledon Champion.'

According to Marcus Jones at Devizes Tenterden: 'We're looking at a test case. The police are telling me that an Indian film star going by the name of Karan was arrested very recently on suspicion of attempting to coerce the tennis authorities into definitely appointing Jon Smartson as umpire for the ladies' final. They are also questioning Karan about the death threats Miss Fleming received during these Championships. More significantly, we want to know why the tennis establishment didn't replace Mr Smartson as the appointed umpire for the final because they were put on notice, by Karan's conduct, that obviously there was a bad intent connected with the proposed appointment of Mr Smartson.

'We believe that the officials have been at least negligent in allowing Mr Smartson to umpire the final and that Mr Smartson himself was at least negligent in overruling his linesman at match point. The smash was in. We can prove that to anyone. And my client, Miss Fleming, has suffered provable direct losses in consequence, such as millions of dollars in sponsorship money. I have thought about sports litigation for many years, ever since my football team Lincoln City lost a cup tie against Crystal Palace due to a "goal" scored about seven minutes into injury time.

'Now we hope that we can finally get justice for Holly Fleming. After all, it was - it has to be said - a remarkably powerful smash.'"

Epilogue

Below are snippets from the posthumous autobiography *Javea Recalled*, edited by Terry Proudley:

"Drew L Todd promised me the world and yet his values were sadly warped. If money had been my only motivation I would never have been a tennis player. No-one can play all those junior matches and practise with nobody watching, year after year, unless they truly have a passion for the sport.

But Drew believed that I was in the game purely to become a money printing machine. He never realised that playing tennis with bravery and flair, and inspiring the gallery, meant so much more to me than my latest deposit account.

Don't get me wrong, money is a motivator but dreaming of pound signs does not create a Wimbledon champ. There are too many years of lonely dedication to go through to hold on to the notion that you're going to be the one in billions who ultimately is kissing the trophy on Centre Court.

So he never understood me, and so I never opened up to him. I became very secretive. And he was so self-absorbed that he completely missed the telltale signs that I was massively in love with Lisa. And around that time I questioned why Drew's clients didn't include any of the smart upcoming black players. You have to conclude what I was able to clarify first-hand, namely that Drew consented with those corporates who were deeply prejudiced against black athletes and failed to give them their due. Of course, it doubly hurt me because Lisa meant life to me, and Drew's conduct basically was a negation of that fundamental truth of mine. So I have no respect for him and after reading this, hopefully you won't, either. In many ways that man wrecked my life."

"Jacalyn Jeanice is a special girl who deserves great happiness. Maybe my life would have been easier if she had been the one for me. Of course it was an ego boost to be so revered by one like her. I saw how all the guys fell over themselves to meet her and yet it was kinda weird because she was courageous enough to make it crystal clear to me that I was her target. But I didn't believe I was great enough to be a sex symbol and I felt that, anyone who was so sure I was, had to have some type of flaw to be thinking that way. The sad part was that, having someone so positive they wanted me, led me to de-value them. If I didn't think I was precious, it was all wrong for someone else to decide that I was the best thing since sliced bread. From there, everything snowballed. She, perhaps to her credit, tried harder and harder to be perfect and romantic towards me, and yet I resented the excessive efforts she was making. So it all went askew. I could have handled it better but I kept hoping she would give up of her own volition. I felt bad about it because it became a silent battle of wills and I won in the end. You get this feeling about some people that they'll never be happy, no matter what happens to them. I hope I am very wrong about Jacalyn Jeanice, because she is a good person and good people should always prosper."

"No doubt you're curious as to how I came to know that Karan, Blanca Alessandra and Jon Smartson planned to cheat tennis completely. It was all by chance, like so much of life. They had been travelling in a tournament courtesy car, the three of them, naively thinking their driver knew no English. But he did. And I was the next guy in his car. End of story."

"There are some people whom you are just destined to disappoint. You look back on it later and you wish you'd never met them because they never meant enough to you to make sure you did the right thing by them. For me, Adele Schmidt is an example of that. I under-estimated her scary desire to win just one Grand Slam title. Yes, I pulled out from the mixed, but my shoulder was in agony that day. The trainer put his thumb into my muscle and I was in so much pain I almost hit the roof! And so Adele will always say I let her down. But all I can say in response is name me one player these days that would rate singles glory as less important than the doubles. Adele always did have a problem with facing reality."

"To my mind, I'll be a brilliant tennis coach once I retire, just like the late great main man, Stan Power. It's not arrogance speaking, I can just see how to beat nearly anyone on the circuit, especially when it comes to the women. In my view, you win matches there by playing the other girl from side to side. Too many of them play hesitantly and diffidently, up and down the middle of the court, whereas the key to success is swinging the ball from left to right and as close to the lines as possible. Other ingredients are a good second serve and the ability to use variety. Why do they rely on power? You win at tennis by mixing topspin and slice on your backhand, and the women's game needs to relearn the art of the dropshot, I'm telling you. What I would do is drag the other girl to the net with killer dropshots and once she's scrambled forward and given me a soft reply, I'd either pass her or do the business with a subtle lob. How many times did we see John McEnroe ignore a passing opportunity and instead opt for the unexpected diagonal lob? The dude was a genius at all that. Dust down the tapes from Wimbledon '84, I say!!

In fact, the way to beat my off court partner Holly Fleming lies in the lob. I have tried to teach her, but she still reacts with leaden feet to a well-timed lob. She's slow off the blocks, fails to get her shoulder facing the net and it's not pretty. One day, I have told her, it'll cause you to lose a major like Wimbledon. Because, at the end of the day, her footwork is poor in response to a lob - and that is no way at all to hit the smash!"

Afterword

"Hi, my name is Pilar Vasquez. The writer of this book made contact with me recently, saying that on the afternoon of Monday, 30 June 1980, when he was 10 and I was 17, I signed an autograph for him on the main concourse of Wimbledon's All England Club. I was in the junior event that year, and went on to have a successful pro career, reaching, for instance, the last 16 at the US Open in 1983, where I only lost to Martina Navratilova. It's so nice that, through James' novel, a chance encounter lasting a few seconds in 1980 has reunited us all these years later. "The Smash!" reminded me of the splendour of Wimbledon, and how happy I am that I played there."

James Harbridge, author of The Smash!